Maggie, Too

OTHER YEARLING BOOKS YOU WILL ENJOY:

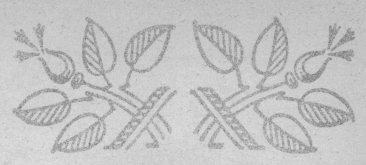

Maggie, Too

JOAN LOWERY NIXON

A YEARLING BOOK

Published by
Dell Publishing Co., Inc.
1 Dag Hammarskjold Plaza
New York, New York 10017

Yearling ® TM 913705, Dell Publishing Co., Inc.

ISBN: 0-440-45288-0

Reprinted by arrangement with Harcourt Brace Jovanovich, Publishers

Printed in the United States of America

August 1987

10 9 8 7 6 5 4 3 2 1

CW

For Allyson
with my love

Maggie, Too

1

Margaret Ledoux scraped the thick, yellow hollandaise sauce off her asparagus and tried to sneak a quick glance at her father through the barrier of red carnations that centered the restaurant table. Something was going to happen that she wouldn't like. Her father was fumbling with his fork and breaking his roll into little crumbs on his bread and butter plate and laughing too loudly with everyone who stopped at their table to say hello or congratulate him on the reviews of his new film. She was sure that he was planning to have another serious talk with her. She wondered what she had done now.

She felt uncomfortable as he watched her, his bald head gleaming in the candlelight, his glasses slipping on his nose. He pushed the glasses back in place with one finger and said, "You're twelve years old, Margaret. You're too big to be playing with your food."

"I'm not playing with it. I hate hollandaise sauce."

"How can you see what it is? Can't you wear a ribbon or a barrette or whatever it is girls wear to keep their hair out of their eyes?"

"I don't like asparagus, either."

Her father sighed. "We've started off on the wrong foot again, haven't we?"

Margaret put down her fork and made an attempt to brush her straight brown hair away from her face. "I don't know what you want, Daddy. I've been home from boarding school almost a week with only Mr. and Mrs. Ellison at the house, and I haven't even seen you, and—"

"You know I had to go out of town. You *know* that."

"Okay. I don't want to argue with you. I just mean that you suddenly come home and say I should dress up because we're going out to dinner. Then you act all nervous and funny, like you do each time you tell me the school doesn't want me back; only this semester I didn't do anything to make anyone mad. I just hate the school. I hate everyone there. But that's no crime."

He sighed again, a sigh so dramatic that Margaret clamped her teeth together to keep from saying something that would only get her into trouble.

"Maybe you'd be happy at school if you really tried to make friends," he said. "Maybe if you lost a little weight or did something with your hair?"

She tried to keep her face like a mask so he wouldn't see how much he had hurt her. Her voice came out barely above a whisper as she asked, "Is that what you want to talk to me about—how you don't like the way I look?"

"Oh, Margaret," he said. "We've never had an easy time of it, have we? I guess it's my fault. I haven't known how to father you, let alone mother you, but I've tried my best. Maybe someday you'll understand that."

A tall woman in a heavily beaded dress swooped down like a gigantic blue butterfly, kissing in the direction of Roger's forehead. "Darling, you're going to get the Oscar for direction on this one. You know you will!"

A short, bubbling conversation, a kiss blown at Margaret, and the woman was gone, leaving the odor of her sticky-sweet perfume.

Margaret's father leaned his elbows on the white cloth, getting as close to his daughter as the table would allow. "I love you," he said, "and I want to make things easy for you. That's why I want to talk to you about Kiki."

Margaret shook her head. "Don't bother. I know about Kiki. 'Twenty-year-old starlet's great romance with her director, Roger Ledoux, old enough to be her father.' We get newspapers at school, too, Daddy. I've known about Kiki—and the others."

He didn't answer for a few moments, but finally he said, "Kiki is different. I'm going to marry Kiki."

Margaret's mind was like a gaping hole. She couldn't speak. The thoughts weren't there. She could only stare at her father while his words tumbled out.

"I wish you could have known your mother, Margaret. The accident . . . I wished at the time that I could die, too. But life has to go on, and marrying Kiki doesn't mean that I love her more than I loved Jeanne. Kiki—well, she's a lot like Jeanne was. She's funny and bright. She loves life and—"

Margaret put up her hands to stop the words. "No! Don't try to tell me how Kiki is like Mother. I don't want to know." Her voice was hard. Her father looked so unhappy that she felt guilty and tried to soften what she had said by adding, "I'll guess I'll meet her before the wedding. Right?"

"Of course! Tonight! Well, no, tomorrow. You see, I told Kiki I'd talk to you about it tonight, so she's expecting to meet you tomorrow."

A couple paused at their table, murmuring compliments about the new film. Roger introduced them to Margaret, and she tried to respond, but her smile was as stiff as stale toast.

The couple moved on. Margaret looked at her father and knew, with a cold feeling in her stomach, that there was more to come. "Tell me the rest," she said.

He blinked and pushed his glasses up again. "You're perceptive—like your mother was." He took a long breath and said, "I'd like to have you at the wedding, Margaret. More than anything, I wish you could be there. But Kiki and I will be on location in Italy for three weeks, and she wants to be married there."

"So I'm not invited."

"It's not that. I hoped you'd understand about that and about where you'll be."

Margaret realized she was beginning to be afraid. She gripped the edge of the tablecloth, twisting it in her trembling fingers. "Tell me where I'll be," she whispered.

"I'm trying to!" He cleared his throat and said, "You have to understand that Kiki is very young. She wants our marriage to be a success as much as I do, and she doesn't think she has the ability to deal with a twelve-year-old girl."

"Does she want to send me to camp for six weeks?"

"No," Roger said. "Margaret, we're—well, we're selling the house. I think you can understand how Kiki feels about all those memories of your mother. We'll live in the beach house for a while, until we find something larger. That beach house, as you well know, is much too cramped for three people, so you'll be spending the entire summer—until school starts—with your grandmother Landry in Houston."

Unshed tears burned Margaret's eyes, and the back of her throat hurt. "I don't even know my grandmother!"

"She writes to you. A few times she's phoned, when she's known where you were."

"But that's different! I've never met her!"

"Margaret, don't raise your voice. People are looking at us."

Margaret glared at her father, her anger holding back the tears. "You want to get rid of me, so you're sending me to live with someone who's practically a stranger—anything to keep me out of your life. Okay. I won't bother you. I won't bother Kiki. I don't even want to meet Kiki. I want to go to Houston tomorrow morning."

Her father's voice was soft and sorrowful. "All right. If that's what you want, Margaret. This has been difficult for both of us, and I hope you realize that I did my best in trying to tell you."

The waiter appeared at her father's side and gave a crisp little bow. "Is everything satisfactory, Mr. Ledoux?"

"Uh, yes. Of course." He waved the waiter away.

Margaret shook her head, and the tears broke loose, rolling down her face, hot against her skin. It no longer mattered to her who was looking or what they thought. "I don't care if you want to get married, Daddy. And I've always known that you really didn't know what to do with me, which is why you've always sent me off to boarding schools. But I'll never be able to forgive you for being such a coward that you had to bring me to a public place to tell me all this. If we had been at home, we could have tried to talk about it."

"I—I was afraid you'd be upset, and I didn't want—"

Margaret pushed back her chair and stood. "Come on, Daddy. The longer I'm in Los Angeles, the more it's going to hurt both of us."

"Margaret," he said.

But she rushed out of the restaurant, elbowing past the starch-coated waiters and narrowly missing the chocolate-curled, whipped cream-swirled creations on the pastry cart. Whatever else her father had to say, Margaret didn't want to hear it.

✻ 2 ✻

It didn't take long for Margaret to pack. She pulled her suitcase out of the closet, opened it, and tossed in all the things she thought she'd need. Then she added the small Walkman radio and earphones she always had at hand. Her radio could help her shut out the world. With music going through her head during the worst times, she didn't feel so much alone.

She snapped the suitcase shut. It was late, but she couldn't make herself go to bed. She prowled through the house long after her father had retired, wandering from room to room, stroking the back of a familiar chair, touching the dark wall paneling as though she were saying good-bye to the only home she had ever known.

"What am I doing?" Margaret murmured as she entered the living room and turned on the nearest table lamp. The decor was pale blues and creams and crystal, with carpets so thick the room was like a whisper. Margaret thought of this as her mother's room because of the small portrait of her mother that hung over the Grecian fireplace. She had always felt that her mother—so lovely

7

and elegant in the painting—matched this lovely and elegant room.

As Margaret looked at the painting, she realized what must have been at the back of her mind, why she hadn't been able to sleep. She padded across the thick carpet to the fireplace, stretched on tiptoes, and took down the portrait of her mother. She guessed that, with the frame, the painting was about sixteen by eighteen inches. It would easily fit in her suitcase. Her father had always treasured this painting, but he didn't deserve to have it now. Kiki would undoubtedly want to toss it in the back of some closet, and he'd probably let her. Margaret clutched the frame as angry tears burned her eyes. Too bad for both of them. She was going to steal the painting.

Margaret's alarm clock woke her in time for her early flight to Houston. She stumbled through the last-minute preparations and a quick toast and orange juice breakfast. Neither she nor her father seemed to be able to think of the right things to say, so the ride to the Intercontinental Airport was, for the most part, a silent one. There was a frantic search for a parking space, a sprint down the long crowded corridors to the right gate, and a breathless pause as Margaret was issued a boarding pass.

Her father turned her over to a flight attendant, who put her in a line near the boarding door with four younger children who were flying alone. "Stay here while I make the announcements," the attendant said. "I'll board you in just a minute."

The terminal was crowded with chattering people. Roger cleared his throat a couple of times, glancing around impatiently, as though he wished everyone would go away, and finally said, "Have a good summer, Margaret. I'll miss you."

Margaret just stared at him.

"Look," he said. "I know you don't understand, and I must have made a mess of telling you about—about my plans. But I'm trying to do what is best. You realize that, don't you, Margaret?"

The attendant appeared and took the hands of the two youngest children. "All right. Let's go!" he said.

"I love you, Margaret," her father said.

The hurt and anger had turned into a hard lump, squeezing out all other emotions. She didn't feel any love for her father. She wondered if she ever had. For an instant she wished she really knew what it was like to love someone so much that it felt happy and warm and right. Maybe she'd never find out.

Margaret looked at her father without caring or feeling. "Good-bye, Daddy," she said. She ran to catch up with the flight attendant.

As soon as Margaret fastened her seat belt, the little boy sitting next to her said, "I'm going to visit my dad. Are you going to visit your dad or your mom?"

"Keep quiet," Margaret mutttered. "I don't want to talk to anybody right now."

It wasn't until the plane was close to Houston that Margaret began to think about her grandmother Landry. She had some snapshots of Grandma and Grandpa Landry taken two years ago, just before Grandpa had died; and each year she had dutifully sent Grandma one of those little school photos, so she suppoosed they'd have no trouble finding each other in the airport. Grandma's letters had always been friendly, but she had no idea what her grandmother was really like. It didn't matter. At the moment she didn't care.

A voice came over the intercom: "We're approaching Houston and will be landing in approximately ten minutes.

If you want to change your watches to central time, it's 3:20 P.M. Our pilot has turned on the no-smoking sign. Please fasten your seat belts, return your seats to the upright position, and make sure that your tray-tables are securely in place."

Margaret glanced out the window. They were flying at a much lower level. Only a few wispy clouds marred a vista of flat green fields cut with lakes and meandering rivers. The plane flew lower and lower, over a thick forest, until suddenly a landing strip appeared, and in a short time they had taxied to one of the terminals.

As the plane stopped, Margaret took a deep breath and wondered why her hands were trembling. Okay, so she would manage to live through a dull summer with a pleasant—she hoped—elderly grandmother, go back to a miserable boarding school in the fall, and hang on until she was old enough to make her own decisions. Then she'd go someplace as far away from her father and Kiki as possible and live her own life.

The flight attendant already had the two small boys in tow. "Come with me," he said to Margaret. He smiled. "And welcome to Houston."

As Margaret left the boarding tunnel and quickly glanced at the people waiting to meet the plane, she had the terrifying feeling of being deserted. There was only one woman who looked like a grandmother, and she was rushing with open arms to enfold the two boys.

But someone touched Margaret's shoulder, spun her around, and said, "Oh, Margaret! I'm so glad you're here!"

Margaret found herself facing a tall, slender woman with red-brown hair, green-gold eyes, and a smile that was big enough for two people. "Grandma?" she gasped.

Grandma laughed. "I forgot you'd have that old picture of me. Well, honey, I got contacts and touched up my hair a little. I just don't feel like gray hair." She took a step backward and examined Margaret. "Oh, my, you're beautiful, Margaret, and so much like your mother was. I knew you would be."

Someone jostled Margaret, and she nearly dropped her handbag. The movement broke the spell this surprising grandmother had cast. Margaret impatiently shook her long hair back from her face. "Don't tell me lies just to try to make me happy," she said. "My mother was beautiful, and I'm not. In case you haven't noticed, I'm twenty pounds overweight, and I've got gross, straight hair."

"I wasn't comparing you with your mother when she was a grown girl and went off to Hollywood looking like a beauty queen. I'm saying that you look just like your mother did when she was twelve. She carried some extra pounds, too." Grandma grinned. "And she complained that her straight hair was 'yucky.'"

Grandma put one arm around Margaret's shoulders, guiding her toward the walkway into the terminal. "Don't look at me so suspiciously, young lady. I'll prove it to you. I've got a big baby book filled with pictures of Jeanne growing up. If you like, I'll even give it to you."

Margaret stopped, excitement making it hard to breathe. She wanted to say, "Yes! I'd love it!" But the lump of anger and hurt kept her from saying anything.

"Come on now, honey," Grandma said. "Let's go get your luggage and head for home."

The warm outdoors air was a shock after the air-conditioned terminal. "Is it always this hot in Houston?" Margaret asked.

"You're just getting a sample of summer," Grandma said. "July and August will be even hotter. But you'll get used to it."

Margaret didn't want to get used to it. She was tired of getting used to new places—and people she didn't know.

There was almost too much for Margaret to absorb on their ride from the airport. They drove on a series of freeways that had as much traffic as the Los Angeles freeways. Downtown Houston's tall, mirrored buildings gleamed like a set for a science fiction movie, but when Grandma turned off the freeway at Shepherd and headed north, the buildings became squatty and old and nearly hidden by garish signs. Grandma glanced at Margaret as though she could read her mind. "I don't like the looks of this street either," she said, "but we've got to drive it to reach my neighborhood."

She turned left, then right, down streets with older brick houses, many of them decorated across the front with broad, covered porches. She pulled into the driveway of a dark red brick, two-story house and turned off the ignition. "Here's home, Maggie," she said.

Margaret stiffened. "Nobody calls me that," she said. "I like to be called 'Margaret.'"

"Sorry," Grandma said. "My name's Margaret, you know, and—"

"I didn't know," Margaret said. "I guess I just thought of you as Grandma."

"Well then, that makes us even. Since everyone calls me 'Maggie,' I took it for granted that you'd be 'Maggie,' too."

"We don't know much about each other, Grandma."

"Never you mind, Margaret," Grandma said. "We're going to have a nice quiet summer to get acquainted."

They dropped Margaret's bags just inside the front door, and Grandma took Margaret on a tour of the house, ending in an upstairs bedroom with wide front windows and white wallpaper sprigged with tiny blue flowers. A puffy white eyelet comforter was spread across the mahogany poster bed.

"This was Jeanne's room," Grandma said. "I thought you'd like it."

Margaret's fingers tingled as she lightly touched the flowered wallpaper. "Did she choose this?"

"Oh, no. That paper's been changed a couple of times since Jeanne was your age. It was yellow then, a sort of buttercup design. She liked everything bright and cheerful. I bet you're like that, too. Are you?"

Before Margaret could answer, someone began pounding on the front door and jabbing at the doorbell at the same time.

"My gracious!" Grandma said. She made a dash for the stairs. Margaret ran with her.

Grandma threw open the front door. On the porch stood a woman with scraggly blond hair that hung over her eyes. She carried a pair of towheaded little girls, one under each arm, balanced on her hips. "Miz Landry," she said, "could I come in?"

"Why, of course," Grandma said. She stepped aside and, as the woman hurried into the entry hall, added, "Gloria, I'd like you to meet my granddaughter Margaret. A few weeks ago Gloria and her children rented half of the duplex next door, and—"

Gloria shook her head as though she were shaking away the introduction. As the woman's hair flew back, Margaret could see that fear had pulled her mouth into a tight grimace. "Miz Landry," Gloria interrupted, "could you lock the door? A man with a gun's in my house. He's lookin' for someone that he said used to live there. And he told me he's gonna kill me!"

3

Grandma quickly locked the door and turned to Gloria.

"Did you call the police?"

"I didn't have a chance. He sat down, mumblin' somethin' to himself, so I grabbed the kids and lit out the back door and ran over here. I don't know if he'll figure I'm here or not."

"Then call the police now. There's a phone in the kitchen. Margaret will take care of the children."

Margaret's knees felt like the rubbery gelatin served in school lunchrooms. She wanted to run, to hide, but Grandma was matter-of-factly pulling the shades over the narrow windows on each side of the front door.

The children began to whimper. Their blue eyes were wide, and they stared at Margaret like little owls. She reluctantly reached out and gripped their hands. "Come upstairs with me," she said. They didn't move, so she added, "I've got some candy in my handbag."

With one accord they lunged toward her. Gloria put them down, and Margaret led them up the stairs.

"What are your names?" she asked.

They didn't answer, but Gloria called, "The big one's Annie Sue, and the little one's Bonnie Joy. They don't talk much yet."

Margaret couldn't tell which was older. They were both pretty small and about the same size. She led them into the bedroom and over to her sacklike, tan leather handbag, where she liked to keep what she thought of as emergency rations, and pulled out two packets of candy. She glanced around the well-cared-for room. Thank goodness this candy was the kind that's not supposed to melt in your hands.

The children were still staring with wide eyes. "Which one of you is Annie Sue?" Margaret asked.

Neither answered, so she held out one packet of the candy and said, "Annie Sue first. Hold out your hands."

One of the towheads immediately reached for the candy. "Now we've got that straight," Margaret said. She tore both packets open and handed one to each of the little girls. She listened for any kind of sound coming from downstairs, but the house was unnaturally quiet. If that man came after Gloria with a gun and started shooting, could a shot reach them upstairs?

"Let's play it safe," Margaret told the children. "We're going to sit on the floor on the other side of the bed. Isn't that fun?"

They followed her obediently as they solemnly chewed the candy, plopping themselves down without saying a word.

"Don't you ever say anything?" Margaret asked them, but they simply stared back at her with the same wide-eyed expression. Margaret shivered, wondering what would happen next.

15

She heard the sirens first, then the screech of tires in front of the house. When a deep, amplified voice called, "Police. Come out without your weapons," Margaret jumped. The voice was loud enough to be coming from inside the room.

"Stay right here and don't move," she whispered to the children, wondering why she was whispering. She crawled to the window that overlooked the front yard and carefully peered outside. "Oh, no!" she cried. "They've got the wrong house!" She tried to open the window, but it held tightly, glued in place by many coats of paint.

Someone had seen her. An arm pointed at her window, and some of the helmeted heads that bobbed up and down behind the police cars turned in her direction.

"Send out your hostages," the voice on the bullhorn boomed.

With a screech two panel trucks marked with television channel symbols skidded to a halt behind the police cars, and men jumped out, pulling cables and cameras.

Margaret took one quick look to see that Annie Sue and Bonnie Joy were where she had left them, then raced down the hall and down the stairs, nearly bumping into her grandmother. "The police think it's this house!" Margaret shouted.

"I figured as much," Grandma said. She looked at Gloria. "Did you give the police this address?"

Gloria shrugged. "I don't know. I guess. They asked where I was calling from. Should I go out and tell them?"

Grandma frowned. "No. I don't want you outside. What if someone starts shooting?"

"Where are the kids?" Gloria asked.

"They're sitting on the floor upstairs in the second room, behind the bed, eating candy," Margaret answered.

Before she had finished the sentence Gloria was halfway up the stairs.

"You stay here, Margaret," Grandma ordered. "I'll just phone the police and straighten it out that way." She hurried toward the kitchen.

Margaret peeked through a slit she made by pulling aside one of the window shades, but in no more than a couple of seconds heads turned in her direction, and the amplified voice called, "Send the children outside."

She let the shade drop quickly and leaned against the wall. In the kitchen Grandma seemed to be arguing with whoever was on the other end of the telephone line. The police began barking orders on the bullhorn again, and Margaret couldn't stand it any longer.

She opened the door and edged out slowly. She could see the tips of rifles aimed at the house. "Don't shoot! I'm only twelve years old!" she yelled, and raised her hands in the air.

A voice from the bushes below the porch said quietly, "Keep coming, honey. Just keep walking."

"Okay," Margaret said as she walked across the porch to the top of the steps. "But I've got to tell you something."

Without warning, someone the size of a football player leaped from the bushes, swooped her up, and ran with her to a spot behind one of the police cars. She found herself sitting on the street with three uniformed officers crouched in front of her.

"Are you all right? Who else has he got in there? Has anyone been hurt?"

Margaret tried to catch her breath as another rapidly fired question hit her. "What can you tell us?"

"That you've got the wrong house!" She explained that Gloria had given the wrong address.

"So which house is he in?" one of the officers asked.

"Grandma just said 'next door,'" Margaret said. "I'd better ask her."

Before anyone could react, she jumped to her feet and ran up the walk. "Hey!" someone yelled, but she leaped up the steps and raced across the porch and into Grandma's house.

Grandma was just coming from the kitchen. "I hope I've got that straightened out," she said.

Margaret was breathless. "Which house does Gloria live in?" she panted.

"Why, that one." Grandma pointed toward the west. "Margaret, I don't understand—"

Margaret threw open the door, pointed, and yelled, "That one!" and slammed the door.

"What in the world?"

"Grandma," Margaret said, "I have to tell you something."

But there was a commotion outside. Grandma pulled up the shades, and they saw an unkempt, staggering man being led to a police car.

"He gave himself up," said the policeman who came to Grandma's door a moment later. "Now, where's the lady who called us?"

Everything seemed to happen at once. Gloria was interviewed by the television people, who crowded into the entry hall, some policemen questioned Gloria and Grandma, and Annie Sue and Bonnie Joy began to cry.

"He might get awful mad at me if they put him in jail," Gloria said. "Next time, he might come back lookin' for me!"

Bonnie Joy wailed so loudly that Margaret couldn't hear what the others were saying. In desperation she picked her up, and immediately Annie Sue clamored to be picked up, too. Their sobs subsided to runny-nosed sniffs and snivels, and Margaret's shoulders grew damp. "Yuck!" she muttered. "I'll be glad when your mother takes you home!"

"I don't think that man will come back," Grandma said to Gloria. "From the looks of him, I doubt if he even knew where he was. Besides, I'm sure he'll be spending some time in jail."

Gloria held out her arms for her children, but Grandma put a hand on her shoulder. "Leave them with us," she said. "Margaret and I will take care of them while you get a little rest. You're still trembling and ought to lie down."

"You mean we have to baby-sit?" Margaret asked, but Grandma ignored her.

"They'll be wanting to eat somethin' pretty soon," Gloria said.

"What do they eat?" Grandma asked.

Gloria shrugged. "Anythin' and everythin'. Are you really sure you want to watch them?"

"We'd love to," Grandma said.

Margaret felt irritated at suddenly finding herself a baby-sitter when all she wanted was the chance to be alone for a while, but Grandma seemed to be waiting for her to say something pleasant. Quickly she blurted out, "How old are your children?"

"Two."

"They're twins?"

"No. Annie Sue's an old two, and Bonnie Joy's a new two. They're ten months apart."

Grandma shut the door as Gloria returned to her own house. She leaned against the wall and studied the children. "Well, Margaret," she said with a smile, "we've got an old two and a new two to take care of. How do you like the start of our quiet summer together?"

"I don't," Margaret said. "I didn't plan on being a baby-sitter."

"Too bad you don't like the job," Grandma said, "because you're good with the twos. You took care of things very nicely while all that fuss was going on."

One of the twos grabbed a fistful of Margaret's hair, and Margaret grimaced. "As usual, I guess I don't have a choice about what I do. I warn you, Grandma, I don't know anything about baby-sitting. Besides giving them candy, what do you do with little kids?"

"First you wipe their noses and wash their faces and change your blouse while I make a couple of phone calls. Then we all walk down to the boulevard for pizza—with lots of pepperoni."

The pizza was good. They all—including the twos—ate as though they were starved, and Grandma told growing-up stories about her children that made Margaret laugh, even though she didn't want to. She was still laughing as they walked back to the house. The western sky was light with far-off pinks and blues, but deep shadows had settled over the porch and yard. Down the block, the streetlights blinked on.

Margaret held both the twos as they climbed the porch steps, so Grandma could fish in her handbag for the front door key.

"Momma! Where were you?"

The voice from the depth of the porch startled them, but as a tall, muscular, dark-haired man stepped out of the shadows, Grandma said, "Oh, thank goodness it's only you, Dennis. Come and meet your niece Margaret."

Margaret had opened her mouth to say hello when a huge dark shape appeared behind Dennis. The twos shrieked, and Margaret screamed as it leaped at them.

4

"Flowerpot!" Dennis yelled. He tugged and grunted and managed to halt the beast, but not before it had given a rough, wet swipe of its tongue across the faces of Margaret and both the twos.

"Yuck!" Margaret yelled. She hugged the twos tightly.

Grandma said, "It's all right. Don't be afraid. See— Uncle Dennis has the bear on a leash."

"It's not a bear, Momma," Dennis said.

"I suppose it's not a hairy moose, either," Grandma said, "although it's big enough to be one."

"She's a dog," Dennis said. "Let's go inside where there's more light, and I'll introduce you to Flowerpot."

Flowerpot eagerly bounded into the house, dragging Dennis with her. The others entered reluctantly.

"Sit," Dennis said to Flowerpot.

She jumped up and slobbered happily as she licked his face.

"You stupid dog! Sit!" he shouted.

The dog slowly settled to the floor, spreading out like

a shaggy rug. Dennis tried to wipe his face with the back of one hand.

"Maybe she thought you said 'spit,'" Margaret suggested. It was mean to laugh, but she couldn't help it.

Annie Sue pointed at Flowerpot and giggled. Bonnie Joy looked at her sister and giggled, too.

"Well, now that your dog has brought a ray of sunshine into our lives, maybe you'd like to keep her in the backyard while you're here," Grandma said to Dennis.

"She's not my dog. She's yours," Dennis said.

"No, thank you," Grandma said.

Dennis persisted. "She's a present from me to you and Maggie."

Margaret interrupted. "I wish people wouldn't call me Maggie. My name is *Margaret*."

"Oh," Dennis said. "You were named after Momma, so I thought you'd be called Maggie, too."

Grandma shook her head. "As for your furry present, Dennis, again my answer is no, thank you."

"Aha!" Dennis exclaimed. "You may turn down your half, Momma, but it would be rude for Margaret to refuse to accept a present from her loving uncle."

"Put Flowerpot in the backyard," Grandma ordered. "Then tell me what you're up to."

Dennis tugged and pulled on Flowerpot's leash. When the dog finally got to her feet, she bounded beside him on the way to the kitchen. There were a few bumps and thumps before the rest of them heard the back door slam.

Dennis joined them in the den and sat on the sofa across from Grandma.

"You didn't ask who our short friends are," Grandma said.

"I didn't have to. I saw them on TV, and I can guess you're taking care of them until their mother recovers."

He leaned toward his mother, resting his elbows on his knees. "Janet and Sharon and I have tried to get you out of this neighborhood and into a high-rise apartment with good security, but you won't listen to us. So, since you insist on staying here, I've bought you a watchdog."

"I don't need a watchdog—especially one named Flowerpot. Suppose a robber does break into the house, and I yell, 'Attack, Flowerpot!'"

Margaret said, "It might work. The robber would probably die laughing."

Grandma chuckled, and Dennis grinned at Margaret. "Hey, you're a lot like your mother. She could always come up with a funny punch line."

Margaret just smiled. She didn't think she should tell them that she never thought of anything funny. She'd been as surprised as anybody else by what she had just said.

There was a knock on the door. Grandma was just getting out of her chair to answer when the door opened, and a voice called out, "It's me, Gloria. Can I come in?"

"You see why you need a watchdog? You didn't even lock the door, Momma!"

"I couldn't climb over that hairy elephant to get to the door!"

Gloria came into the den. She looked at Grandma. "I couldn't sleep," she said. "I've never been so shook up. I just hope they keep that awful man in jail." She began to sniffle.

The twos looked at their mother and wailed.

With a crash, the back door burst open. Flowerpot ran through the kitchen and into the den.

"Uh-oh," Dennis said. "I forgot that the latch on that door needs fixing."

The dog paused to take in the scene, then poked her large nose into Gloria's face before anyone could stop her.

"No, Flowerpot!" Dennis yelled, but Gloria simply stopped crying and rubbed her cheek against Flowerpot's shaggy head.

"Good doggie," she said. "Sit."

Flowerpot sat.

Gloria stroked Flowerpot's head. "I once had a dog like this, only he was white instead of black, and he was little, and he didn't have much hair, and he was real scared of people, so he'd hide under the bed if anybody came to the house."

Margaret could see that Grandma and Uncle Dennis were as puzzled as she was. She thought that someone ought to say something, so she asked, "What kind of a dog was he?" She let go of the squirming twos, who ran to their mother's lap and solemnly began to pet Flowerpot.

"Anybody's guess," Gloria said, "which is like this dog. She's an anybody's-guess kind of dog, too."

"Oh." Grandma sounded relieved. "Well, you're very good with her."

"Yeah," Gloria said. "Dogs like me." She yawned so widely that she reminded Margaret of a baby bird waiting for dinner.

"You've had a hard day," Grandma said.

"Yeah," Gloria agreed. "I better take the kids home now and put them in bed. It's gettin' late."

She managed to stagger to her feet while holding both the twos. Dennis gripped Flowerpot's collar with both hands, but Gloria just put her fingertips in front of the dog's nose and said, "Stay."

Except for her drippy red tongue, which was hanging out of her mouth, Flowerpot did a good imitation of a statue. Dennis cautiously released her collar.

"Remarkable," Grandma said, and she walked to the

door with Gloria. "If there's anything else we can do for you, just speak up."

The moment the door shut, Flowerpot began to race around the room. "Sit!" Dennis yelled. "Stay!" Margaret shouted. But Flowerpot ignored them.

"Put that dog outside!" Grandma's voice rose over the commotion. "And this time make sure that door will stay closed!"

"I'll play out there with her," Dennis said, "so she'll feel welcome in her new home." He managed to catch Flowerpot and drag her toward the open back door.

Grandma dropped onto the sofa next to Margaret. "I haven't given up on our first quiet evening," she said. "After Dennis goes home to his apartment, you and I can make some tea or cocoa, and talk. If you'd like to talk about your mother, we can do that."

Margaret did want to talk about her mother, but there was something she had to find out first. She blurted out a question that had been pricking like a sharp needle: "Why didn't you ever come to see me?"

"We did! Honey, we came when you were a new little baby, and the next year Jeanne brought you to visit us here in Houston."

"I didn't know that!"

"Sure. And we saw you again when we went out to Los Angeles after—after the accident."

Grandma stopped, and Margaret said, "But you didn't come to visit when I was old enough to remember. Why?"

Grandma thought for a moment. Then she looked at Margaret and said, "I wrote more than once to invite you to come to visit us."

"But it was always when I couldn't," Margaret said. "Like the summer Daddy sent me to board in Switzerland, or when he wanted me to learn French in Paris." She paused. "It was Daddy, wasn't it?"

Grandma patted her hand. "Margaret, I—"

Whatever Grandma was going to say was lost when a voice called from the direction of the front door, "Momma! Are you there? Are you all right?"

"Sharon?"

Grandma jumped up just as a slender, pale woman ran into the room, arms wide, and enfolded her in a hug. With her red hair and freckles, the woman looked so much like Grandma that Margaret would have recognized her aunt anywhere.

Before Grandma could say a word, Sharon had rushed to hug Margaret, too. "Oh, little Maggie! I'm so glad to finally meet you!"

Margaret's face was squished against her aunt's shoulder, but she managed to snap, "I'm *Margaret*."

"Of course you are, dear." Her aunt held her at arm's length and studied her. "But what a terrible way to be introduced to Texas! You must tell me all about it, Maggie! And we're counting on you to help talk your grandmother into moving to a nice, safe place where—"

"Sharon, slow down," Grandma interrupted. "You weren't listening. Margaret likes to be called Margaret—not Maggie."

Sharon's eyes opened wide. "Oh. Well, whatever. I just took it for granted she'd be Maggie, too. I mean, when—"

"Sharon," Grandma said, "I'm glad to see you, but I wasn't expecting you. I thought you and Andy planned to drive here to meet Margaret at the end of the month." She turned to Margaret. "Sharon and Andy live in Austin. It's about three hours from here."

"I was listening to the car radio and got the late afternoon news and heard what happened to you and called Andy at his office and told him I was coming straight to Houston as soon as I could throw something in the suitcase, and called my boss and he gave me my vacation time now, so here I am."

Margaret let out a long breath.

Grandma giggled, winked at Sharon, and said to Margaret, "Sharon affects people like that, but don't think you have to breathe for her. She manages all right on her own."

Sharon sighed. "I don't know why I get so wound up," she said.

"Maybe to keep the conversation from running down," Margaret said.

Sharon gently held Margaret's face between her hands and beamed at her. "Isn't she witty? What a darling! Just like Jeanne!"

Margaret wished she could tell this babbling aunt that she was trying to be sarcastic, not witty. Before Sharon could say another word, the doorbell rang.

"What in the world?" Grandma said.

They all went to answer it and found Gloria, her arms filled with the twos, a teddy bear, a small pillow, and a few blankets. "You said if I needed anythin' to just ask you," Gloria explained. Her lower lip quivered. "Well, I'm scared over there. I hear noises. If it's all right with you, could we sleep at your house tonight?"

5

Grandma bustled around, mumbling to herself under her breath. Sharon was assigned to the bedroom she had once shared with her sister, Janet; Gloria and the twos got the flowered sofa in the den that suddenly became a pull-out bed; and Dennis was told to go home.

"But Flowerpot stays here," Dennis insisted. "I brought a bag of dog food and some dog dishes, and I'll put them in the kitchen with her. I want her to sleep inside." He tried to look stern and added, "So she can protect you."

Grandma waved a hand. "All right. I don't feel like arguing about it right now." So Dennis settled Flowerpot for the night and left, saying that since the next day was Saturday, they'd see him early.

Margaret found herself holding an armful of sheets, so she made the sofa bed and tucked the twos into it before anyone got the idea that maybe they should sleep with her.

"Okay," Grandma said as she came back to the den. "Everybody seems to be taken care of."

"Grandma," Margaret asked, "were you ever in the army?"

Grandma laughed. "No," she answered. "As you know, I'm a school librarian, but sometimes I think both jobs have a lot in common."

Margaret had forgotten about her grandmother's job. She tried to imagine her grandmother outside the context of being just Grandma, and she couldn't. She suddenly realized, with a shivery feeling at the back of her neck, that she knew almost nothing about her grandmother Landry, that she was still a stranger in a strange—and noisy—house in a strange city. And there was nowhere else she could go. She wasn't like some of the girls she had known at school or at summer camp, who had looked forward so eagerly to going home. She didn't have a home, and with her father's plans, she wouldn't even have a house to go home to.

Grandma wrapped her in a hug that smelled of both perfume and pizza. "You look tired, honey," she said. "Why don't you go on up to bed? Would you like me to take your suitcase upstairs?"

"Thanks, but I can do it," Margaret said. She attempted to respond to her grandmother's hug, but she wasn't used to hugging people, and she felt stiff and uncomfortable. Grandma didn't seem to notice. She just gave Margaret a quick, extra squeeze and made a dash for Bonnie Joy, who had climbed out of bed.

It didn't take Margaret long to get ready for bed. She slid between the cool, smooth sheets in the bed that had once belonged to her mother and felt a familiar ache in her stomach. Even the steamy-hot shower hadn't helped. Margaret tried to think about her mother and the house in which she had grown up, but she couldn't. She had never felt so much alone. *What difference does it make*? she told herself. *I came here planning just to kill time, didn't I? So why should I expect things to be any different?* She didn't understand why she suddenly felt so miserable.

Even with her bedroom door shut, she could hear the sounds from downstairs. Someone had turned on the television set in the den, and one of the twos was crying. Margaret put her fingers in her ears, then had a better idea. She climbed out of bed, found her Walkman, and got back into bed with the earphones on.

Snuggled into the pillow, with the blanket up to her chin, she turned the dial, trying to find the kind of station she wanted. Country western, another country western— then there it was, just the right kind of music. Margaret settled back to listen.

At the end of the record the deejay said, "So—which one of you will be the winner of our all-expense-paid, two-week trip to the beautiful ocean shores of Cancun, Mexico? Soft, rolling surf, balmy beaches, terrific food! Just print your name, address, and phone number on a postcard and send it to Cancun Holiday, KIFF, P.O. Box 2222, Houston, Texas 77832. Enter as often as you want. We'll draw some lucky person's card on June thirtieth—just one week and one day from now—and give them five minutes to phone in. You may be our winner, so do it! Send in your card today!"

Margaret sat straight up in bed as he repeated the address. She threw back the blanket and wanted to shout. That disc jockey was talking to her! What a great idea! She could win that trip and go away from *everyone*. She'd like to be by herself. She'd enjoy those balmy beaches and the terrific food and all that peace and quiet.

Margaret removed her earphones and flipped off the radio. She turned on the small bedside lamp, crawled over the foot of the bed, scrambled for her handbag, pulled out a pen and a scrap of paper, and wrote down the address.

Then she tugged her wallet from the bottom of the bag and counted the money her father had given her. He didn't expect her to spend much. What he had given her was more of an emergency fund, because if a problem came up that demanded more money than she had, like a trip to a doctor, his secretary would just send a check to whoever needed it.

Could she spare twenty-five dollars out of her funds? Why not? She'd buy twenty-five dollars' worth of stamped postcards at the post office, fill them out, and send them in. That many postcards would give her a much better than average chance of winning.

She turned off the radio and scooted down into the pillows, but before she could turn off the lamp, there was a soft tap at her door.

It opened a crack, and Grandma peeked in. When she saw Margaret looking at her, she smiled and walked over to the side of the bed. "Comfortable?"

Margaret nodded.

"Mind if I sit down?"

Before Margaret could tell her she did mind, Grandma perched on the edge of the bed. "I got to thinking about the two-hour time difference between Los Angeles and Houston and how it's only eight o'clock there, so you're probably not sleepy. Am I right?"

Margaret wanted to enjoy the secret and excitement of the trip she was going to win, not sharing her thoughts with anyone; so she faked a yawn and said, "It's been a long day."

"Are you hungry for a snack?" Grandma asked.

"No," Margaret answered, but her stomach—as though it were answering for itself—gave a long, low growl.

The corners of Grandma's mouth quivered. Margaret knew her grandmother was trying not to smile. Finally she said to Margaret, "Gloria and the twos are asleep, but I can't sleep. All this commotion around here has been driving me bananas, and when I'm going bananas, I want to eat ice cream. I sent Sharon to the boulevard to get caramel pecan ice cream sundaes for the three of us. It's not too hot out, so we'll eat them on the front porch."

"No, thank you," Margaret said. She immediately wished she hadn't been so stubborn because, in the long pause that followed, she could practically taste that ice cream.

Grandma looked down at her hands. After a moment she raised her head and smiled at Margaret. "Honey, a while back you asked me a question about your father, and I didn't answer it."

"It doesn't matter," Margaret said quickly. "I don't want to talk about my father. Not right now."

Grandma patted Margaret's shoulder. "All right, Margaret." She stood and walked to the doorway. When she turned to face Margaret, her voice was cheerful. "I'm so glad you're here. Remember now, if you get hungry or lonely, come on downstairs and join us."

"I'm used to being lonely," Margaret murmured. Her grandmother didn't answer. She just left the room and went down the hall as though she hadn't heard. Margaret wondered if she had said the words aloud. She hoped she hadn't.

She tried to pull back the thrill of the balmy beaches that were going to be hers, but it had gone. Instead, she thought about her grandmother and the caramel pecan sundaes and how she really wasn't sleepy yet and how boring it was to just lie in bed.

Margaret went downstairs and out to the porch.

Grandma spoke from the darkness. "Over here, Margaret. There's lots of room on this swing."

As Margaret approached Grandma and Sharon, her eyes grew accustomed to the dark. She sat down between them and accepted her carton of ice cream and a spoon. She wanted to apologize to Grandma, but all that came out was, "I guess I was hungrier than I thought I was."

"We're glad you joined us," Grandma mumbled with her mouth full. "This stuff is so delicious it's a crime."

"Margaret," Sharon said, "we need your help." She licked her spoon and continued. "I've been telling Momma that if she's not going to be sensible enough to sell this house and move to a security apartment, then she ought to accept Flowerpot—although I don't know who could give a dog such a ghastly un-dog kind of name—and let her protect her. Don't you agree? Don't you think that Flowerpot will grow on her?"

"I don't know," Margaret said. "I think it's more likely that Flowerpot will sit on her."

Grandma let out a whoop of laughter, then covered her mouth with her hand. "I didn't mean to wake the neighbors," she said.

"Are there any left who aren't inside your house?" Margaret asked.

Grandma chuckled. "You have a great sense of humor!" she said.

Before today, no one had ever told Margaret that. Someone was usually telling her that she was too serious, or too withdrawn. She decided not to mention that to her grandmother.

Not only was the ice cream wonderful, but Margaret also felt pleased with her newly discovered sense of humor. And she thought it was fun to sit outside in the dark in her nightgown. Unseen crickets chirped down in the shrubbery, and the flowers on a vine that twisted around a nearby brick pillar smelled even more delicious than the ice cream.

For a little while, she forgot about the feelings that had been such a pain in her stomach.

But Sharon sighed. "I'm serious, Momma," she said. "We're all worried about you. We wish you'd be sensible and move. You tell her, too, Margaret."

"Do you really want my opinion?" Margaret asked.

"Of course we want your opinion," Sharon said.

They both looked at her. Margaret gave a last lick to the ice cream spoon and said, "It's hard to leave a house and know you'll never live in it again. I know. Lots of times I'd come home from boarding school or camp, and my father would be away on location, and only Mr. and Mrs. Ellison, who work for my father, would be there. So I never thought much about the house. I never knew I'd miss it until my father told me he was going to sell it. And then I felt sad because there were lots of things to remember in that house. Grandma has lots of things to remember in hers."

Grandma reached over and squeezed Margaret's free hand. Sharon sighed. "Well, as you said, Margaret, that's only your opinion."

An automobile pulled into the driveway, the beams of its headlights sweeping across them. All three turned to see a woman jump from the driver's seat. She called, "Momma! It's me!" She waved a small box in the air. "I brought you a burglar alarm!"

6

"Janet?" Grandma sounded astonished.

"Hey, Sis!" Sharon said. "So you made it, too!"

"You bet! I drove up from Corpus Christi the minute I saw the early news!"

Grandma climbed out of the swing and peered over the railing. "Where are John and the children?"

"John couldn't come. He has to operate tomorrow. But Debbie and Jason are with me. They fell asleep. Does somebody want to come down here and help me carry them?"

They were all inside the house, each carrying the box, a suitcase, or one of the children, before Grandma was able to say, "Janet, this is Margaret."

Janet was tall and slender, with short, dark hair. She looked like Dennis, Margaret thought, and probably like Grandpa. Janet's children had dark hair, too, and although their faces were scrunched against the adults' shoulders, she could tell that they were very much like their mother. Debbie seemed to be mostly dangling, skinny legs, and Margaret sighed, wishing she could have inherited 'thin,' too.

Janet stretched to peer at Margaret over her armful of sleeping son, and smiled. "We couldn't wait to meet you, Maggie!"

"Margaret," Grandma, Sharon, and Margaret said together.

"What?" Janet blinked and looked from one to the other.

"Margaret likes to be called Margaret," Sharon explained.

"Oh. Okay. I thought that because she's named after Momma, she'd be Maggie, too."

Sharon tried to shift Debbie in her arms and groaned. "My arms are breaking. Why do children weigh so much more when they're asleep?"

"Maybe because they're heavy sleepers," Margaret said. She put the package she'd been holding on the hall table.

Sharon groaned at the pun, but Grandma laughed and Janet beamed. "Oh, Margaret," Janet said, "you've got your mother's marvelous sense of humor!"

Sharon staggered toward the stairs. "Momma, tell me quick! Where do you want me to put this heavy child?"

"Well—" Grandma looked at Margaret. "It's just temporary, Margaret, but would you mind if Debbie shares your bed tonight? Since it's a double bed, there should be plenty of room."

Sharon started up the stairs. So did Janet. No one had waited for Margaret's answer. She supposed no one cared what she thought. Why did Grandma ask if she didn't want to know? Margaret hated the idea of sharing her bed with a six- or seven-year-old little kid, but she really didn't have a choice. Grandma was already telling Janet that she could take the other twin bed in the room with Sharon, and she'd make a pallet on the floor for Jason.

"What about the sofa bed in the den?" Janet asked.

"It's already occupied," Grandma said. "Sharon will tell you all the details. Oh—and don't go in the kitchen. She'll explain that, too."

Grandma turned out the downstairs hall light and climbed the stairs behind Margaret. She put down Janet's suitcase and followed Margaret into her bedroom. Bending over Debbie, who was curled into a ball, she tucked the blanket over her shoulders. "Grandma's little love," she whispered.

She straightened and turned to Margaret. "Hop in, and I'll tuck you in, too."

Margaret stiffened. Of course Debbie would be Grandma's little love. Jason, too. She was with them often, and she loved them. They weren't here just because their father wanted to get rid of them, the way she was.

"No, thank you. I have to brush my teeth." Margaret knew she sounded formal and stiff, but she couldn't help it. She walked into the bathroom and began noisily scrubbing at her teeth. Margaret wiped her face on a towel and stared into the mirror. She told herself it wasn't Grandma's fault that a granddaughter she didn't know had been dumped on her. She didn't understand why she felt so mad and mixed-up. The image that looked back at her didn't have the answer, either.

"Cancun," Margaret whispered to herself, hoping the magic word would help, and went to bed.

Debbie not only rolled over next to her, but she also kicked out every once in a while, whacking Margaret in the leg. Margaret moved so close to the edge of the bed that she nearly fell out; but the sleeping Debbie, who breathed in a steady, rattling sniffle, moved with her.

Carefully, Margaret eased out of bed and got back in on the other side, sighing with relief, thankful for the room she had in which to stretch out. But along came Debbie, snuffling and snuggling like a bear cub searching for the warmest spot in the cave.

Margaret gave up. *Cancun, Cancun,* she thought over and over until she finally fell asleep.

She dreamed there was an earthquake, and all the buildings were falling down. She was in school, but the people running past her were strange creatures from another planet, and everyone was screaming. A bucket of warm water hit her in the face.

Margaret sat up in bed and shoved at Flowerpot, who was licking her nose. "Get off the bed!" she yelled. The twos were downstairs, screaming and crying. It had to be more than just the twos making that much racket.

Flowerpot leaped off the bed with a thud that seemed to shake the room, and raced out into the hall. There was just enough daylight to see the clock. Five forty-five! Margaret ran down the stairs.

Jason and Debbie were standing on the dining room table. Gloria was trying to round up both the twos, and Flowerpot was galloping through the rooms as though this were the best game she'd ever played.

"If you grab Flowerpot, I'll take care of the children," Margaret shouted to Gloria.

Gloria clutched Flowerpot's collar on the dog's next turn through the room and said, "Sit."

Flowerpot sat, panting, with her long tongue hanging out and fluttering like a small red flag. The children stopped crying.

"What is that?" Jason asked, pointing at Flowerpot.

His sister stared at Margaret. "Who are you? Do you belong to him?"

"I'm your cousin Margaret," she answered. "And that black thing is only a dog named Flowerpot. Uncle Dennis gave it to Grandma to be her watchdog."

Grandma, Janet, and Sharon came hurrying down the stairs. Janet had some pink stuff on her face, and Sharon clutched her robe to her throat. Grandma, whose hair was standing up in a tangled mess, was still tying the belt on her robe. Everyone began talking at once.

"Who opened the kitchen door?"

"We wanted something to eat."

"Get off the table! You know better than to stand on the table!"

"Could we have pancakes?"

"Yes, Grandma will make pancakes if you stop pulling on her robe."

"Where did Dennis find such a monstrous dog?"

"Gloria, you're so good with the dog, do you think you could get her to go outside?"

"Mama, somebody was in bed with me when I woke up. Was that Margaret?"

"Are the Saturday cartoons on TV now?"

"Didn't you hear me tell you to get off that table?"

Margaret went upstairs again, and no one noticed. She shut the bedroom door and climbed back in bed, snuggling down on her stomach and pulling the pillow over her head. It was only four in the morning California time. If they were going to eat pancakes this early in the morning, they were all crazy. It was nice to have the bed to herself. Everybody else could eat pancakes. She was going back to sleep.

When the knocking woke her, Margaret thought it was someone at her bedroom door. She ignored it, hoping whoever it was would go away. But even from under her pillow, she could hear excited voices, so she rolled over, sat up, and listened.

"Bonnie Joy," Grandma was saying, "turn the little knob. See the little knob, honey?"

"It's no use," Gloria said. "She's crying so hard she can't hear you."

"Maybe if you jiggle the doorknob—" Janet suggested.

Margaret opened her door and found everyone jammed in the hallway around the door to the bathroom.

Jason saw Margaret and shouted, "Bonnie Joy locked herself in the bathroom!"

"You did that when you were little," Debbie said. She giggled.

"I did not!"

"Did too! And Daddy put a screwdriver in a hole in the doorknob and fixed it so you could come out!"

"Unfortunately," Grandma said, "we don't have that kind of doorknob."

Margaret asked, "Grandma, will the bathroom window open?"

"Yes," Grandma answered, "but it's a small window. I don't think any of us could get through it."

"What about me?"

"You? Yes, you could, but that's a second-story climb."

"Don't you have a long ladder?"

"Sure we do, Momma," Janet said. "And we can steady the ladder. Margaret will be all right."

So Margaret quickly pulled on her shorts and blouse and sneakers. She ran past Gloria, who was trying to console Bonnie Joy, to the spot outside the house where the others were putting the extension ladder in place.

She climbed the ladder carefully. It wobbled now and then, and Sharon punctuated each wobble with a gasp or a strangled shriek. It was kind of scary, but Margaret knew she could do it. And she felt pleased that she had come up with the only idea that would work.

The window lifted easily. She poked her head through and smiled at Bonnie Joy, who was standing in the middle of unwound rolls of toilet paper. The little girl stopped crying and stared at her. "I'll have you out in a minute," Margaret said.

First she had to decide how to get into the bathroom. If the sink had been under the window, it would have been easy, but there was a straight drop down to the toilet. "Bonnie Joy," she asked, "can you put the lid down on the toilet?"

Bonnie Joy just stuck her thumb in her mouth and continued to stare.

The window was too small to permit Margaret to pull both her legs through at one time. She felt above the window. The old, wooden window frame was wide enough for her to get a good fingertip grip. She slowly turned, clung to the top of the window frame, and pulled herself to a sitting position on the sill, her back to the room. Carefully, she swung inward and sideways and managed to work her right leg into the room. She was pulling her left leg through the window when she suddenly felt a strong tugging on the right one.

"No, Bonnie Joy!" she yelled. But the little girl was hanging on tightly.

"Bonnie Joy, let go! I'm going to fall!"

Margaret managed to swing her left leg free just in time. She landed on both feet, but the left one ended up in the toilet. Bonnie Joy had stepped back at the last moment, so Margaret was the only one who was drenched.

"My best sneakers," she muttered at Bonnie Joy.

"Open the door!" Gloria shouted, so Margaret dripped

her way across the carpet of toilet paper and opened the door.

Everyone crowded around, hugging Bonnie Joy and Margaret.

"Grandma said you were brave!" Jason shouted over the din.

They were all so busy talking that Margaret was the first to notice. A terrible, burned smell was creeping through the hallway.

"Something's burning!" Margaret said.

The others stopped in midsentence and stared at her.

Sharon sniffed the air and gasped. "Oh, no! The house is on fire!"

7

"It's Jason's fault!" Debbie shrieked. "He wanted to make some more pancakes."

"Everybody outside!" Janet ordered.

Grandma didn't say a word. She made a dash for the stairs.

Margaret was right behind her. While Grandma turned off the stove and dumped the blackened contents of the griddle into the sink, Margaret threw open the kitchen window and the back door to let the smoke out.

Flowerpot bounced into the room.

"Out!" Margaret pointed at the backyard, but Flowerpot ignored her and ran straight through the house and out the open front door.

"We'd better find the others and tell them everything's under control," Grandma said.

"I hear sirens," Margaret said.

The two of them ran to the front porch. A small crowd had gathered on the lawn. Debbie and Jason were playing chase around and between the neighbors' legs. Janet and

Sharon were holding the twos. Gloria had a firm grip on Flowerpot.

"I called the fire department," Gloria shouted to Grandma.

"But there's no fire!" Grandma called back. The siren on a hook and ladder truck that was rounding the corner drowned out her words.

Two smaller trucks were right behind the ladder truck. Firemen jumped from the trucks and set to work.

Grandma ran toward a fireman who was hurrying toward her.

"It's not a fire!" she explained. "We just burned some pancakes."

He turned and shouted to the other men. They stopped what they were doing and waited, watching Grandma and Margaret. Everyone seemed to be watching Grandma and Margaret.

An old lady, with wispy white hair that stuck out in tufts from under a ragged, straw sun hat, hobbled out of her house across the street and shouted from her front porch, "What are y'all up to now, Miz Landry? What's all that racket about?"

Grandma waved. "Everything's all right, Mrs. Fiddy."

"This used to be a quiet neighborhood," Mrs. Fiddy yelled.

Someone in the crowd chuckled. A couple of people smiled. Margaret didn't think that either burned pancakes or Mrs. Fiddy were that funny. She started to say so, but Sharon suddenly rolled her eyes and headed straight toward Margaret on the porch.

"Would you like us to check out the house?" the fireman asked Grandma.

"You don't need to," she said. "It was just some burnt

pancakes. They're already down the disposal. I'm terribly sorry that we troubled you."

"Margaret!" Sharon hurried up beside her and whispered in her ear, "Get in the house."

"Why?" Margaret asked.

"Look at your left foot!" Sharon hissed.

Margaret looked down to see streamers of toilet paper wrapped around her wet sneaker.

Someone in the crowd snickered. She knew it was because of her.

"I'm going to die," she said. Her face was so hot that her scalp felt prickly. As the fire trucks drove off with a clatter and a roar, Margaret turned and ran into the house.

Grandma was right behind her all the way upstairs and into the bedroom. When Margaret plopped on the edge of the bed, Grandma sat beside her.

"What do *you* like to do when you're going bananas?" Grandma gave a long sigh. "The ice cream store isn't open yet."

Margaret held her hands to her cheeks, wishing the burning would go away. "I'm going to take a bath," she said. "Then I think I'll go back to bed and stay there the rest of the summer."

"Bed sounds more comfortable than the closet."

"The closet?"

"Whenever something embarrassing happened to your mother, she'd say she was going to live in the closet," Grandma explained.

Margaret tried to think of the graceful, lovely woman in the portrait ever doing anything embarrassing. She realized she must have looked puzzled because Grandma said, "Once, when your mother was about thirteen or fourteen, we all went to a big party given by your grandpa's company.

They had a drawing for prizes, and one of them was a size-able gift certificate at the best department store in town.

"We were standing near the back of the ballroom when the master of ceremonies called out the winning number. Jeanne screamed and waved her ticket in the air. She had to work her way through the crowd to get to the stage, and all that time, the announcer kept telling people to 'make way for the little lady.' Well, she finally got up on the stage, out of breath and still waving that ticket. The announcer read it, then said there was a mistake. The last in the string of numbers he had read was 'eleven,' but Jeanne had thought he'd said 'seven.' And a lot of people laughed."

"How awful!" Margaret said.

"After she made her way back through the crowd, she told us she wanted to go home and live in the closet."

Margaret giggled. Grandma did, too.

"You can look back on things like that, and they turn out to be funny," Grandma said.

Margaret looked down at her left foot and laughed. "I guess it is funny. I just wish it had happened to someone else."

"I think I'll go jogging and let someone else make your breakfast," Grandma said.

She got up and was at the door before Margaret asked, "Grandma, would you take me to the post office today so I can buy some postcards?"

"I'll be glad to. But wouldn't you rather get some picture postcards at the drugstore?"

"No," Margaret said. She didn't want to tell anyone why she needed the cards.

Grandma didn't ask. She just smiled and left the room.

Margaret hurried through her bath and got dressed in record time. She realized how hungry she was when she sat down to the pancake and bacon breakfast Janet had kept warm for her.

Grandma, wearing a faded purple jogging suit, poured herself a cup of coffee and sat across from Margaret at the kitchen table.

"If you've noticed, the house is a lot more quiet," Grandma said. "Gloria took the twos to their day-care center before she went to her job at the supermarket. And Debbie and Jason are watching Saturday morning cartoons." She took a careful sip of the steaming coffee. "So, little granddaughter, we've finally got a chance to visit."

At that moment Sharon came into the kitchen. "Momma, could I talk to you?"

"How about later?" Grandma said.

Sharon's voice was plaintive. "I've been waiting and waiting for things to quiet down."

"Why don't you sit with us and have a cup of coffee?" Grandma asked.

Sharon made a choking noise. "I couldn't. The smell of the food—I'd get sick again."

Grandma got to her feet and put her hands on Sharon's shoulders. "Honey! Are you going to tell me you're pregnant?"

"Yes!" Sharon exclaimed. "Isn't that wonderful?"

Grandma hugged Sharon.

"We're so excited," Sharon said. "Andy's going to call his parents today and tell them, and I just couldn't wait to tell you, and Janet is going to scream when she finds out, and— Oh, Momma, I really think I'd better get out of the kitchen!"

Sharon ran out of the room. Grandma hurried after her.

Margaret finished her breakfast, licking the last bit of

syrup from her fork. She heard Janet's squeals of delight. She wondered what she should say to Sharon. Best wishes? Good luck? I hope you don't throw up again?

Margaret rinsed off her dishes and put them in the dishwasher. If no one else was going to do them, she supposed she'd have to. She headed for the babble of voices, wishing that they'd all go home and hoping that Grandma would remember to take her to the post office.

When she joined the women, who had gathered in the entry hall, Janet hugged her. "Did you hear the great news about Sharon? Isn't it wonderful?"

Margaret nodded, and the others went on talking until the front door banged open and Dennis staggered through, his arms full.

"What in the world have you got there?" Grandma asked him.

"My sleeping bag, some clothes, and a few other things I'll need." He dropped them in a heap at his feet and added, "Oh, yeah, my dirty laundry, too. I thought I'd wash it here."

"What's this all about?" Grandma asked.

Dennis's voice grew deeper and solemn as he said, "Momma, I did some checking on that guy who threatened Gloria with a gun. They call him Bubba Gletz, and according to a policeman who's a good friend of mine, the guy has been bad news for years, mean as sin and always trying to get even with someone."

"But he's in jail," Grandma said.

"Not anymore, he isn't," Dennis said. "A couple of hours ago, his parents paid his bail and got him out."

8

Sharon and Janet began talking at the same time. Finally Grandma said, "Hold it! I can't think with all the noise you're making. We'll just tell Gloria to stay over here with the twos for a while, and we'll—"

"With the what?" Sharon interrupted.

"Of course you wouldn't know," Grandma said. "Gloria told us that Annie Sue is an old two and Bonnie Joy is a new two, so Margaret and I call them 'the twos.'"

Margaret liked being paired with Grandma in something that was just theirs. It made her wish all the more that the others would go away.

Grandma continued. "Dennis, you can stay if you wish, but I don't think it's necessary."

"I do, Momma."

Dennis sounded so decided that Grandma just shrugged. "All right," she said. "We'll bed you down in the kitchen with Flowerpot."

"Momma!"

"Just kidding." She giggled. "We'll worry about where to put you later. Right now, Sharon has some good news to share with you, and Margaret and I have to get to the post office before it closes."

Margaret ran for her handbag and joined Grandma in her car.

Grandma maneuvered out of the driveway before she spoke. "I think you're smart, getting postcards to write to your father and your friends. Lots of people—unless they're crazy about writing letters, which most people aren't—keep putting it off because it seems like too much of a chore. With postcards the whole thing gets shorter and easier."

Margaret didn't say anything. She didn't want to deceive her grandmother, but she didn't want to tell her about the contest.

"Your father will be glad to hear from you, honey," Grandma said. "He misses you."

"He doesn't miss me!"

"It may not seem like that to you now because you're trying to get used to his marrying again, but he does miss you and love you, Margaret. You're his only child."

"That doesn't mean anything!" Margaret turned to face her grandmother. "He gets rid of me whenever he can. I spend most of my time in boarding schools and summer camps while he's going all over the world."

"Isn't most of that traveling because of his job? Doesn't he have to go on location with the film companies?"

"I suppose so," Margaret mumbled. "But you don't understand."

"You're right. It is hard to really understand other people's problems, no matter how much we love them," Grandma said. "Apparently you and your father are having a hard time understanding each other."

"Grandma, you didn't come to see me after my mother died because you didn't like my father. Isn't that right?"

Grandma turned left onto a busy street and for a moment concentrated on getting into the right lane. Then she said, "It was another case of not understanding. Jeanne was so young, and your father was so much older and had been married twice before. We wanted Jeanne to be happy, and we couldn't understand that she *was* happy—with your father. Naturally, he didn't feel at ease with us when he knew we were against the marriage. I can't blame him."

"But what about me, when I was born?"

Grandma reached over to pat Margaret's knee. "Ah, now, you were really special."

She drove into the parking lot of the post office and parked. Turning off the ignition, she faced Margaret. "We tried to come to see you after Jeanne died, but our timing wasn't right. When your grandpa had vacation time and we could come to California, your father had to be in Europe. And he discouraged us from visiting when he was away and you were at home with your nursemaid and the servants."

Her voice became softer, as though she were talking to herself. "Once, we came to see you anyway. You were nearly three, and the cutest little girl in the world. But you had the sniffles, and your nursemaid was so fierce we could rarely get near you. We gave up and came home."

"But why did he send me to you now, after all these years?"

"He knew this would be a hard time for you," Grandma answered. "And he knew that I'd love and cherish you, and all that love would help."

Margaret thought a moment. "I don't think you're right. I don't think he cares that much about me."

"You may not like things your father has done," Grandma said, "but for that matter, I don't suppose there are many people who've grown up approving of every single thing their parents did. The thing to remember is that your father is doing the best that he can. If you can keep that in mind, then you can appreciate him for that and forgive him for the things that are hurting you."

"Right now, I don't want to forgive him for anything," Margaret said. "And I don't want to talk about him anymore. I just want to buy my postcards."

The line inside the post office moved about as fast as ketchup from a new bottle, but just before noon, Margaret finally reached the counter and bought her postcards.

As she stuffed them into her handbag on her way to the car, the sky changed to a brighter shade of blue, and she thought she heard a bird singing. She was practically on her way to Cancun!

On the way home, Grandma looked at her watch and said, "When we get back to the house, we're going to find that all those hungry people who ate pancakes so early this morning are starving and will want me to make them something to eat. I can promise you that the minute we walk in the door, one of them is going to ask, 'What's for lunch?'"

A few minutes later, when Grandma and Margaret arrived home, Janet opened the door for them. "Hi," she said. "What's for lunch?"

Grandma groaned and said, "I think I'm going to scream."

Dennis joined them in the hallway. "Why do you want to scream?" he asked.

"Never mind," Grandma said. "It's just something Margaret and I were talking about."

"Okay," Dennis said. "What's for lunch?"

Grandma squeezed her eyes shut and gave a little screech. Margaret burst into laughter.

Jason ran into the room and tugged at Grandma's

skirt. "Grandma, Grandma," he shouted. "I'm hungry. What's for lunch?"

Grandma swooped him up. "All right, sweetheart. Grandma will make you something right this minute."

"I'll help," Margaret said. She was discovering that she liked being with Grandma.

"I'm sure you've got things you want to do," Janet told Margaret. "I'll help Momma. I need to talk to her."

"You come with me, Jason," Dennis said. "I'm working on something that will surprise your grandma."

Margaret quickly went upstairs to her bedroom. Okay. If no one needed her around, she did have something to do. She could fill out her postcards.

She seated herself at the little desk under the window, pulled the stack of postcards out of her handbag, and began to write her name and Grandma's Houston address and phone number on the message side. It took a lot of time to write all that information, and she soon got a cramp in her hand. No matter. It was going to be worth it. Cancun. And if she won this contest—*when* she won this contest—she'd be all by herself on those balmy beaches, far away from her father and everyone.

Margaret put three postcards in the nightstand drawer. Someday she might send them to her father. Not because she wanted to, but because Grandma thought that's what she was going to do. She sat back in her chair, wondering if her father would think about writing to her.

"Lunch is ready, everybody! Margaret! Come to lunch!"

Margaret wasn't hungry, but Grandma's voice was insistent. She opened the door and called, "I'm coming."

With all the printing she had done, she had barely made a dent in the stack of postcards. Carefully, she tucked them into the pocket of her suitcase—the same pocket that held the portrait of her mother. She took out the picture and studied it for a moment. Her mother looked a little bit like Janet and a little bit like Grandma. She wished she had known her mother.

"C'mon, Margaret. Grandma sent me to get you."

Margaret jumped as Debbie spoke from the doorway. She quickly stuffed the picture back into the suitcase pocket, zipped the case shut, and fastened the combination lock.

"What's in there?"

"Some of my things."

"Oh." Debbie didn't seem to care. Her mind was on her lunch-to-be. "Hurry up, Margaret. Everybody's waiting for you, and I'm hungry."

Debbie chattered all the way to the kitchen. Margaret wondered if she had been like that when she was seven. She didn't think so. She remembered her father saying to people, "Margaret is a very quiet child." Well, maybe she was quiet because she had no one to talk to.

Grandma broke into her thoughts. "Here come Debbie and Margaret," she said. "Is everyone on hand now? Why is it that people keep pestering to find out when a meal will be ready, and then when it is, they all disappear?"

Margaret hadn't thought she'd be hungry already, but there were platters of cheeses and cold cuts and crackers and bread slices and pickles and lettuce and tomato wedges, and big bowls of coleslaw and fruit salad.

"It's a do-it-yourself lunch," Grandma announced, taking her place at the head of the table.

"Last one to the table is a—" A horrible clanging drowned out Dennis's words.

"What is that?" Grandma shouted.

"The burglar alarm Janet brought! I installed it this morning!" Dennis yelled. He jumped to his feet. "Someone must have come through the front door!"

9

They scrambled around each other, bumping and tripping in their race toward the front door. The clanging continued, growing even louder and hurting Margaret's ears.

A terrified Jason ran to meet them. He grabbed his mother around the legs and screamed, "I didn't mean to break it!"

Everyone tried to shout over the dreadful sound.

"Thank goodness it was only Jason!"

"I thought he was in the kitchen with us."

"Look. My hands are shaking. I thought that man with the gun had come back."

"For heaven's sake, Dennis, turn that thing off!"

"Mama, are you gonna spank Jason for being bad?"

"Doesn't that alarm have an on-off switch?"

"I don't know how to turn it off."

"Jason, stop crying. Debbie, stop telling him he's bad. He's not bad. He's just inquisitive."

"Read the instructions!"

"Where are they?"

"What does 'inquisitive' mean?"

"Ask me later."

Margaret couldn't stand it any longer. She walked through the door, across the porch, and around to the side of the house. It didn't take long to find what she had been looking for. She opened the breaker box. None of the switches were labeled, so she reached for the master switch at the top and pulled it.

The sudden silence was almost as much of a shock as the alarm had been. Some of the neighbors had begun to gather in front of Grandma's house, and a few were standing on lawns down the block, shading their eyes against the sun, looking as though they were waiting for something exciting to happen.

Mrs. Fiddy leaned against her porch railing. Her straw hat flopped up and down as she yelled, "What's going on over there?"

"It was just a burglar alarm. It went off by accident," Margaret called.

"Humph!" Mrs. Fiddy shouted. "This used to be a nice, quiet neighborhood."

Margaret returned to the house, where the others were gathered around Dennis. He looked pleased with himself.

"You shouldn't have panicked," Dennis said. "I told you I could fix it. I just wiggled this little thing right here."

Margaret said, "Grandma, I found your breaker box and turned off the electricity."

For a moment, everyone stared at Margaret. Then Grandma began to laugh, and they all joined in, even Dennis.

"She is so much like Jeanne," Janet said. "Remember when Sharon climbed the tree in the backyard and got scared to climb down, and we were all under the tree trying to coax her and encourage her, and someone wanted to call the fire department. But Jeanne just got the ladder, put it against the tree, and said, 'Okay, Sharon. Now climb down.'"

Grandma hugged Margaret. "Let's all have lunch. All except you, Dennis. You detach that thing fast and turn the electricity back on. It's going to get hot in a hurry without the air conditioner."

"You don't want him to take it out, Momma," Janet said. "Someday that alarm might save your life."

"Janet, it was nice of you to think of bringing it to me, but the last thing I need is a hair-trigger alarm. Every time I opened the door I'd be afraid I'd rouse the neighborhood."

"We want to take care of you, Momma," Sharon said. She put a hand to her forehead and leaned against the wall.

Immediately, Grandma's arms were steadying her.

"I'm all right. For a few seconds I just got a little dizzy," Sharon explained.

"Come with me," Grandma said, leading Sharon toward the den. "I'm going to tuck you and some nice soft pillows into the recliner chair and bring your lunch on a tray. You've had too much excitement."

"Oh, Momma!" Sharon sighed happily. "It's so good to be here. I do love to be pampered."

The lunch was just as delicious as it looked. Margaret was surprised to find how hungry she was. After they had eaten, she began to carry the plates to the sink and scrape them, but Grandma took them from her. "We'll let Janet take care of these," she said.

"But I want to help," Margaret said.

"You can have a turn tonight. Right now, while we can find a couple of minutes to ourselves, I want to show you your mother's baby book." She took Margaret's hand and led her into a little room off the living room. It was lined on three sides with bookshelves.

"I didn't know this room was here. It's like a small

library," Margaret said. She examined the cluttered shelves, packed to the ceiling with books. "Could I read some of these?"

"Of course you can," Grandma said. "I meant to show you this room right away." She chuckled. "But we were interrupted, weren't we?" She went to the window and folded back the shutters, allowing the sunlight to pour across the thick, padded window seat and into the room. A branch from a climbing, deep-red rosebush stretched across a corner of the window. "This is my favorite room in the house," she added. "On cool days in the fall and warm days in the spring, I like to open the window and let the breeze come in."

"I love this room!" Margaret exclaimed.

Grandma said, "Your grandpa built those shelves. Often, in the late evenings, we'd tuck the children in bed, then come in here to read. The room has a nice, cozy feel to it."

She reached into a deep, low shelf and pulled out a large album, dusting it off. "Here's what I told you I'd show you—the growing-up pictures of your mother."

They settled on the window seat, the book stretched across both their laps. Margaret studied, with wonder, the photographs of her mother, a chubby, wide-eyed baby in ruffles and bonnets. As Grandma turned the pages, the baby girl became a toddler, then a gawky first-grader with a gap-toothed smile.

"On the next page is a picture you'll appreciate," Grandma said, and she turned the page to an enlargement in which a plump girl with long, tangled brown hair leaned from the porch swing.

Margaret gasped as she stared into a face so much like her own.

"Jeanne was twelve in that picture," Grandma said. "Just like you. Didn't I tell you that you were as beautiful as your mother?" She smiled. "Maybe even a little more beautiful. You're fine-boned and graceful, like your father's side of the family."

Margaret couldn't talk. There was too much to think about, too many discoveries to make. It was hard to take her eyes off the girl who looked back at her in the photograph.

Grandma slid the book onto Margaret's lap and got up. "I'm going to check on Sharon," she said. "You just stay here and look through the rest of the book. You'll see the swimming ribbons your mother won when she was ten, and the pictures of her in high school and in a frilly formal at her prom."

The scrapbook gave Margaret a strange feeling. It was almost as though she were getting a preview of the future, seeing what she would be like as she grew up. And for the first time, she thought of her mother as a real person, not simply a beautiful woman in a portrait. Her mother had been a little girl and had climbed trees and roller-skated on the sidewalks and had had a doll collection. And she had lost her baby fat and had curled her hair and had grown up, which was what Margaret had yet to do.

For a while after she closed the scrapbook, Margaret sat with the sun toasting her back, thinking about her mother. Someday she would want to look through these books in the library, some of which obviously had been read and reread until they were shabby. But now she just wanted to sit quietly and think.

Jason came to the doorway. "Hi," he said, holding two metal trucks toward her. "Wanna play trucks?"

"Not now," Margaret said.

Jason got to his knees and, with a truck in each hand, crawled around the room, saying, "Vrooom, vrooom, vrooom."

Margaret put the scrapbook back in its place, stepped over Jason, and went upstairs to her bedroom. Thank goodness Debbie wasn't there.

She opened her suitcase and took out the stack of postcards and her pen. Carefully, she continued printing her name and the rest of the information she'd need on the message side of the cards. She had to get these finished so that she could get them in the mail in time. Margaret could picture the disc jockey reaching into a big sack of mail and pulling out her card. With so many cards, she had a better chance than anyone of winning that contest.

A door opened, and she could hear Grandma and Janet in the hallway.

"I just don't know what to do," Janet said. She sniffled and blew her nose, so Margaret guessed that she'd been crying.

"All I can say is what I told you earlier," Grandma said. "Talk to John. Tell him how you feel."

"He should know how I feel, without being told! How would he feel if I were gone most of the time, and he had to spend evening after evening all alone with the children?"

Margaret tried not to listen, but it was impossible.

"Much of what he's doing is taking care of patients, but you said he works with the civic club. Why don't you get a baby-sitter and go with him to those civic club meetings?"

"Why should I have to do something I'm not interested in, just because he wants to do it? That's not fair."

"Doesn't John sometimes do things you like to do and he doesn't?"

"Oh. Well, I guess so. But that's just once in a while."

Margaret gave a little cough. She hoped they'd hear her and stop talking. She didn't want to eavesdrop. She didn't want to find out about Janet's problems. But they didn't seem to hear her.

Grandma said something, and Janet answered, "Momma, all I want is to just stay here awhile. I want John to be lonely for me. I want him to see how it feels."

"That's not going to solve the problem." Grandma's voice began to fade, as though she were walking down the hall toward the stairs.

For a moment Margaret felt resentful of Janet, who wanted to hide here, and Sharon, who wanted to be petted and pampered, and Gloria, who wanted someone brave to take care of her. Grandma already had a problem dumped on her, a problem named Margaret. How did Grandma feel about having so many problems in her house? Did she secretly wish they'd all leave?

Debbie began to scream, "You can't catch me!" and it sounded like elephants running down the hallway. Doors banged, and Jason screeched.

"I've got to get out of here," Margaret mumbled to herself. She bent over her cards and began to print faster.

🌿 **10** 🌿

Margaret leaned back and rubbed her hand when she finished the last postcard. Now all she had to do was take the entire stack, turn it over, and write the radio station's address on each of the cards. This was hard work. She hadn't known it would take so long to fill out all the cards.

"It's worth it," she mumbled to herself. However, maybe she'd wait until later to work on the cards again. She was awfully tired of writing.

She had just put the postcards back in her suitcase when Grandma tapped on the door and walked in.

Margaret jumped and fumbled with the case, locking it quickly.

"I didn't mean to startle you," Grandma said. She was breathing quickly, as though she'd been hurrying.

Margaret knew she must look as guilty as she felt, but Grandma didn't seem to notice. She just said, "Hurry up, honey. Long distance. Your father's on the phone. You can take it in my bedroom so you'll have privacy."

Margaret slowly got to her feet. "Daddy called me?"

"Yes." Grandma made a shooing motion with her arms.

"Hurry. Don't keep him waiting. Long distance costs money."

Margaret dutifully followed Grandma to her bedroom. There was a puffy, flowered comforter on the bed, and a pair of fat pillows in matching shams rested against a slightly faded, blue, padded headboard. Margaret sat on the edge of the bed and picked up the telephone.

Her hands felt wet and sticky, but her throat was so dry it was hard to talk. She waited until Grandma left and shut the door, then said, "Hello, Daddy."

"Margaret!" Her father's voice was so filled with heartiness and good cheer that he sounded like some of the parents who came to summer camp tournaments to root for their children to win. He wouldn't be that jovial if he had noticed that she had taken her mother's picture, Margaret decided. She sighed with relief and leaned back against the headboard of Grandma's bed, to which clung the faint, spicy fragrance of Grandma's perfume.

"We're leaving for Italy this evening, so I thought I'd call before we go. How is everything? Are you and your grandmother getting along well?"

"She's very nice to me," Margaret answered.

"Has she shown you around Houston?"

"Not much. Just what I saw coming here from the airport."

"Well, of course," he said quickly. "You only got there yesterday. That was a dumb question for me to ask. So— well—nothing much has gone on yet, I guess."

"Not much," Margaret said. There was too much to tell, and besides, he wouldn't be interested.

"Have you got anything planned? Swimming lessons? Anything like that?"

"I already know how to swim," Margaret said. "I thought you'd remember."

"Now I remember. Of course. What are you doing?"

"Talking to you, Daddy."

After she said it, she knew it would irritate him. It just happened to be the first thing that had come into her head. She didn't mean to be contrary, but there was no way she would tell him about Cancun and the trip she was going to win. Nobody was going to know about that until they announced her name over the radio.

There was a pause. Then her father said, "Well, Margaret, I just wanted to make sure that everything was all right and that you were getting settled in for the summer."

"I'm okay."

"And I—uh—thought it might help to have a little talk, since you were upset when you left."

There was another pause. He was waiting for Margaret to answer, but she didn't want to. What was she supposed to say? It's okay, Daddy, for you to send me away because your new wife wants you all to herself and there's no room for me?

"Kiki was sorry she didn't get to meet you," her father said. "By the way, when we get our new house, there'll be a room just for you, and Kiki wants to decorate it herself."

"Gee. Wow," Margaret said.

Her father sighed. "Margaret, don't be difficult."

Margaret spoke in a rush of words, before she could change her mind. "Daddy, I took that portrait of Mother. I knew that Kiki wouldn't want it around, and I couldn't let her just hide the picture in the back of a closet."

"You took it?" There was silence until he said, "Margaret, you know how much that painting has always meant to me."

"To me, too, Daddy. I didn't want Kiki to get her hands on that picture."

There was silence again. Finally he said, "This is no

64

time to discuss it. That painting is also valuable because of the artist. Have you got it in a safe place? Are you taking good care of it?"

"It's in my suitcase."

"Ask your grandmother if she'll let you hang it. Not where it will catch direct sunlight. And not where it will be subject to wide temperature changes. Do you understand how to care for it, Margaret?"

"Yes."

There was another pause. "I've routed our flight home from Italy so that we can stop off in Houston for a day. I'd like to see you, Margaret, and I'd especially like you and Kiki to get acquainted."

Margaret could hear a woman speaking to him, and he said, as though he were trying for some of his original enthusiasm, "Kiki would like to say hello to you now."

Margaret squeezed her eyes shut and gripped the phone. She was so angry she could hardly keep from shouting. "Has she been listening to our conversation?"

"She's simply been here in the room. That's all."

"But she was listening to what ycu said to me! There's no one here with me, Daddy, because I was talking just to you."

"Margaret, be reasonable."

"I don't want to be reasonable. And I don't want to talk to Kiki! And I don't want to meet Kiki! And I don't want to see you, Daddy! Don't come here! I don't want you to!"

"Then we'd better end our conversation." His voice was cold, even though he added, "I love you, Margaret."

Margaret clenched her teeth. She wouldn't say it, and no one could make her. "Good-bye, Daddy," she answered, and dropped the receiver on its cradle.

She brushed the back of one hand across her face,

wiping away the tears, surprised because she hadn't realized she'd been crying. "If he really wanted to talk to me, why did he have Kiki there?" Saying the words aloud made it all seem even worse. She lay across Grandma's bed and cried until she was so tired that the tears dried into small, scratchy lumps in her throat.

The phone rang once. Someone must have answered it downstairs. Margaret sat up, took a Kleenex from the box on Grandma's nightstand, and blew her nose.

The door opened, and Grandma came in. She blinked. "Oh. I thought you were back in your room." She took a long look at Margaret, sat next to her on the bed, and said, "Do you want to talk?"

Margaret shook her head.

"All right, then," Grandma said. She reached over and with her fingertips gently brushed back the straggly strands of hair from Margaret's forehead. "Let me tell you our plans for tomorrow afternoon. We're going to Galveston to go swimming, and before we head back for home, we'll get some shrimp—those nice, big kind—and when we get home, Dennis will barbecue them for us on the outdoor grill. How does that sound?"

"Okay, I guess."

"I'd like to see you swim," Grandma said. "I remember the letter you wrote to me about getting your junior lifesaving badge."

"*You* remembered."

"Of course I did."

But her father hadn't.

Margaret stood. "Grandma, will you come with me? I want to show you something."

She led her grandmother to the bedroom, opened the suitcase, and took out the portrait of her mother. She held it up so Grandma could see it.

"Oh, my!" Grandma's voice was not much more than a whisper. "Oh, isn't that beautiful!"

"I hid it in my suitcase when I came here," Margaret said.

Grandma didn't take her eyes off the portrait. "And?"

"And I just told my father. He hadn't been to the house, or if he had, he hadn't noticed. It was over the fireplace in the living room. I knew that Kiki wouldn't have let him hang it in their new house, so I took it."

Grandma's fingers brushed the top of the frame in the same way she had brushed back Margaret's hair from her forehead. "What did Roger say?"

"He said we'd discuss it later. But he told me to ask you if we could hang it. He asked me to take good care of it—as though I wouldn't unless he told me!"

Grandma walked to the wall at the side of the room, reached up, and took down a framed landscape print that was hanging there. "Here's a good place for the picture of your mother," she said. "It's high enough so the children can't reach it, and you can look at it each morning when you wake up and before you turn out the lamp at night."

She took the painting from Margaret and hung it in place. "How's that?"

"Great," Margaret said. "Thanks, Grandma."

Grandma took a last, long look at the painting. "Your father made your mother very happy," she said, and left the room.

Margaret didn't want to think about what Grandma had said. She didn't want to think about her father at all, so when she heard a commotion downstairs, with Debbie and Jason yelling and shrieking and laughing, she decided to find out what was going on.

❀ 11 ❀

Gloria, flanked by the twos, was holding a gigantic plastic sack of caramel popcorn. It was almost as tall as she was.

"A friend of mine works in a popcorn shop," she explained. "She sold this to me at half price because I told her I wanted to bring y'all a present for bein' so nice to me."

"You didn't have to do that, Gloria," Grandma said.

"Well—I kinda hoped that tonight—"

Grandma patted Gloria's shoulder.. "I was going to come over as soon as I thought you'd be home from work and tell you that I wanted you to stay with us again tonight."

"Really?"

"That guy's out on bail," Janet said.

Gloria's eyes grew huge, and her mouth opened in a large O.

"Don't be frightened," Grandma said. "Frankly, I don't think we'll see him again. He looked so out of it, he probably didn't even know where he was."

"What if he comes back here?" Gloria whispered.

"Well, we've got Dennis and Flowerpot to protect us."

"Don't forget—I took a karate class a few years ago," Sharon said. She reached for the popcorn bag and took it from Gloria. "I think I'll have some of this right now."

"You'll spoil your dinner," Grandma warned.

"Oh, Momma, just a little bit." Sharon sighed. "Being pregnant makes me so hungry."

"Well—" Grandma shrugged. "Take it to the kitchen and have just a taste—and that means you and no one else." She bent down and gave Debbie and Jason a firm look. "I'm making a pot roast with all the trimmings, and I don't want people telling me they're not hungry."

"Pot roast?" Gloria immediately looked happier.

"Yes," Grandma said. "Why don't you get the things you'll need for tonight right now and bring them over here? Margaret will help."

Margaret would have liked to complain about being volunteered without being asked, but instead she reached for the twos and took their hands. Helping would keep her mind off the caramel popcorn. She wished she could think of a good excuse to have some, too, but she couldn't.

They made the move in one trip. Gloria either didn't have much to move, or she didn't want to go back into her empty house again. All the time she was trotting in and out of the bathroom and bedroom, piling clothes and things in Margaret's arms, she was making a little "Oooh, oooh, oooh" sound under her breath.

Margaret put Gloria's possessions in a corner of Grandma's den. Sharon was tucked into her chair again and was watching an old movie on television. The twos sat on the floor to watch with her.

A sharp, piercing noise came from the living room. Margaret stuck her head in long enough to see Debbie and Jason sitting upright in front of their mother with small, wooden recorders in their mouths. Janet was chopping the air with one hand in a kind of rhythm and saying, "One and two and three and four."

Since they were only hitting half the notes, Margaret didn't want to hear any more, so she headed for the library. But Dennis was there, lying on the floor, his head pillowed on his bedroll, watching a football game on a portable TV.

"Hi," Dennis said. "Want to see a really good game?"

"No, thanks," Margaret said. "I don't like football very much. I always think I can hear the players crunch when they fall on top of each other."

At that moment the crowd cheered wildly as at least half a dozen bodies piled on top of the player with the ball.

Margaret shuddered. "See what I mean? Did you hear them crunch?"

She left the room as Dennis repeated to himself, "Hear them crunch? Ugh!"

No one was in the kitchen, but a rich, pungent, spicy beef fragrance was coming from a large pot on the stove. The kitchen was so filled with it, Margaret could practically taste it, and her stomach gave a loud, empty rumble. She knew she couldn't stay in the kitchen and survive until dinner. Okay—back to the bedroom to work on the postcards again.

The door to Grandma's bedroom was ajar. Margaret peeked in. She was about to say, "Grandma? Are you there?" when she saw that her grandmother was sleeping, curled on top of the quilt. She could hear her steady breathing, so she knew she was asleep. Her sandals were lying on the floor, and her bare toes twitched. As Margaret looked at her grandmother, she felt a strange warmth, something she had never experienced before. It was as though she wanted to pat her grandmother, to hug her, to snuggle up against her the way one of the twos might do.

Margaret tiptoed to the bed and pulled the edge of the quilt up to cover her grandmother's feet. Nobody could sleep very well with cold feet. As she left, she shut the door so quietly that it didn't make a sound. Apparently Grandma also needed to get away once in a while.

She went to her own bedroom and stacked the postcards on the desk. She found the slip of paper with the name of the radio station and copied the address. After three or four cards, she was sure she'd remember that address the rest of her life.

Margaret was getting to the point at which her hand ached when there was a tap at the door and Grandma walked into the room. Margaret stiffened, not wanting Grandma to see the postcards. The warm feeling had gone. She was irritated now and wished Grandma would wait to find out if she wanted her to come in.

But Grandma's eyes were on the painting of Jeanne. She didn't seem to notice anything else.

"Some very thoughtful person put the comforter over me," she said. "I bet that was you."

"Your toes were twitching," Margaret said. "I thought they were probably cold."

"So, I have twitchy toes, do I?" Grandma smiled and held out a hand. "I need someone to help set the table and peel potatoes. You can be my volunteer."

Margaret stood up. Why didn't Grandma *ask* her if she wanted to do something? Why did she always have to volunteer her? She didn't smile back at Grandma. She didn't feel like smiling. "You never ask Sharon to do stuff," she said. "I think you're spoiling her."

"Sometimes certain people need to be spoiled a little. Sometimes other people need to keep busy." Grandma cocked her head to one side and studied Margaret. "You aren't used to family life, honey."

"That's because I don't have a family," Margaret said.

"Come on," Grandma said. She put an arm around Margaret's shoulders.

Margaret stubbornly kept her shoulders as stiff as they'd been before, but she followed Grandma to the kitchen.

Dennis came in. "I've been looking for you, Momma. Do you know we're out of cookies? And when is dinner?"

"Soon," Grandma answered. "How's the football game?"

Dennis frowned at Margaret. "Uncomfortable," he said. "I thought I'd get away from it for a little while."

With a clatter Grandma pulled a pot from a cabinet under the stove and half-filled it with water. "You were probably lying in the same spot too long. You need some exercise. Suppose you feed Flowerpot."

"Okay," he agreed and opened the back door. Flowerpot must have been waiting for that moment. With a gigantic leap from the top of the picnic table, she sailed into Dennis and past him, as he staggered against the wall. They could hear her racing through the house with the abandon of a herd of stampeding buffalo.

"Gloria!" Grandma called.

"I'll get her!" Gloria yelled.

It took more than a few minutes because first she had to calm down the twos. Flowerpot seemed to be exploring the entire house, but Gloria finally cornered her upstairs.

"Heel," Gloria ordered, and Flowerpot calmly trotted next to Gloria down the stairs and through the house to the kitchen.

"It's amazing how you do that," Grandma said.

Flowerpot lifted her head and looked as though she smiled under all that hair. But Margaret saw something sticking out of the corner of the dog's mouth. It looked like a postcard!

Without thinking, she put an arm around Flowerpot's neck and pulled the card out of the dog's mouth. "She ate part of my postcard!" she cried.

Gloria nodded. "She got things sort of stirred around in your room. Nothin' broken, though," she added quickly, glancing at Grandma. "She did eat somebody's white sock. She swallowed it before I could get to her."

Margaret didn't wait to hear the rest. She raced upstairs. It had been her own fault for leaving the postcards out and the door open, she knew. But she wasn't angry with herself. She was angry at that dumb dog, especially when she saw that some of the cards had been stepped on and slobbered on.

She picked them up, dried some of them off on her shirt, tried to straighten out the wrinkled ones, and tucked them all back into the suitcase. She'd just have to send them like that. She wasn't going to miss one chance to win that vacation!

The rest of the weekend wasn't much better. The next day, Sharon said she didn't want to go on that long ride to the beach. It was too hot, and she'd get carsick. But she didn't want to stay alone. She wanted Grandma to stay with her so she could ask her all sorts of questions about taking care of a new baby.

The traffic on the freeway was heavy and poky. It took so long to get to Galveston that Jason and Debbie became bored and got into a pinching fight in the backseat of the car. As soon as they arrived at the beach, Dennis cut his foot on a broken beer bottle. Janet drove them to the hospital, where they all waited for hours in the lobby in their bathing suits until Dennis finally got his foot cleaned and bandaged.

"It's too late to go swimming now," Janet said. "We might as well go home."

"It's not my fault," Dennis grumbled. He limped into the front seat beside Janet.

On the way home, Jason and Debbie decided to pinch Margaret. "If you do that once more," Margaret told them, "I'll show you what it's like to really feel pinched. You'll each be nothing but a big blob of purple."

Debbie and Jason immediately sat back against the seat, their hands in their laps.

Dennis chuckled. "That's telling 'em, Margaret."

"Really?" Janet said to Dennis in a voice colder than the inside of the ice chest. "John and I believe that threats have no place in the care and raising of well-balanced children."

Dennis mumbled something that Margaret was glad she didn't hear, and he and Janet argued for the next half hour. Debbie and Jason fell asleep on Margaret's shoulders.

As Janet parked the car in the driveway, Debbie and Jason awoke and, in a whirlwind of sharp elbows and knees, scrambled over Margaret. She groaned, her shoulders stiff from trying not to wake them, and slowly climbed out of the car.

Grandma appeared on the front porch. "Did you have a good time?" she asked.

Jason and Debbie burst into tears and raced to her, grabbing her around the legs.

Grandma patted them, making soothing sounds. Then she looked at Dennis, Janet, and Margaret. "You did get the shrimp, didn't you?"

"Oh, no!" Janet began to cry and ran into the house.

"It's my fault!" Dennis yelled. "They can all tell you that it's my fault we forgot to buy the shrimp!" He limped back to the car. "Never mind that my foot is killing me! I'll go out and get hamburgers for everybody!"

He backed the car down the driveway and, with a squeal of tires, headed toward the boulevard.

Grandma shooed the children into the house and turned to Margaret. "I guess it's up to you to explain."

Margaret was hot and itchy and stiff and wished she could cry, too. "On a scale of one to ten," she said as they walked into the house, "I guess you could say that our trip to the beach was a minus five."

Bonnie Joy came by, clutching something to her chest. Part of what she was carrying fell, and Margaret could see that it was one of her postcards.

She looked up the stairs, right into Jason's guilty face. "I was just playing mailman," he said.

Margaret pulled the cards from Bonnie Joy's tight little fists, ignoring her shrieks, and ran after Jason. Surely nothing else could go wrong!

❧ 12 ❧

All postcards entered in the contest had to be mailed before Thursday, so on Tuesday Margaret worked furiously to finish printing the radio station's address on the last batch of cards. She had worked on them every chance she'd had, but there had been so many interruptions. With so many people staying in the house, sometimes it was hard to find even one quiet, all-alone minute. Grandma had taken to eating ice cream like crazy. Then when anyone wanted her, they couldn't find her because she did a lot of jogging to work off the calories.

Getting everyone to bed each night seemed to be a major project, especially since every now and then after Jason, Debbie, and the twos were finally quiet, Flowerpot took it into her head to race across the backyard, throw herself against the fence, and bark furiously.

Dennis had to climb out of his sleeping bag and search the yard.

"That crazy dog," he'd grumble. "Probably thinks she saw a cat."

Debbie had begun following Margaret like a puppy,

and on Monday, Grandma had taken them all to the Galleria mall for shopping and lunch. Janet had been extra-attentive to Margaret because, as she said, "I'd like to make up for that horrible trip to Galveston." And on Monday night, Dennis had insisted that Margaret go with him to a movie.

Margaret had only about ten cards left to write when Grandma called to her from the foot of the stairs. "The mailman came, Margaret. You have a letter!"

Carefully tucking her cards out of sight, Margaret hurried down the stairs. "Are you sure it's for me?" she asked.

Grandma grinned at her. "Of course I'm sure. It's from your father, and he sent it Express Mail so you'd get it in a hurry."

Margaret took the letter and slowly climbed the stairs. Her father didn't write often. He always complained that he wasn't very good at writing letters; so she didn't expect many while she was away at school. She hadn't expected him to write to her now, especially since he had phoned on Saturday. Maybe that's what this letter was all about. It hadn't been a very happy phone call for either of them. Kiki was probably upset because Margaret wouldn't talk to her. Was the letter going to tell her how wrong she had been?

Margaret sat cross-legged on the floor, with the letter in front of her. She didn't want to open it. Just looking at it made her feel a little scared, a little sick. A lump seemed to press against her stomach. She wished he hadn't called or written. It would be so much nicer to just go away to Cancun without any more problems to face.

She sighed and tore open the end of the envelope. If she had to read this letter, she'd better do it as soon as possible and get it over with.

"Dearest Margaret," the letter began. "When you told

me that you had taken Jeanne's portrait, I was angry because I treasure that painting over everything I have ever owned or ever will own. I loved your mother deeply, and that painting reminded me of the dear and beautiful person she was.

"But I had never thought beyond myself where the painting was involved. I hadn't realized that it meant a great deal to you, also. Jeanne was not just my wife; she was your mother, and a part of your memory must surely retain an awareness of the great love she had for you during the first two years of your life.

"I love you, just as she did, although you and I know that sometimes I do a bad job of showing what I feel. I've tried to do my best as a parent, and I'm sorry for the mistakes I've made. At least I can try to share with you the love I felt—and still feel—for your mother by giving her portrait to you. It's yours now, and I know that as you grow into young womanhood yourself, it will mean more and more to you."

Her first thought was, *You're giving me the portrait because you know Kiki doesn't want to have it in the house.* But she knew that wasn't right. Her father had been writing the truth, and it must have been as hard for him to write this letter as it was for her to read it.

There was another paragraph: "In spite of what you told me, I feel it will be best for you and Kiki to meet as soon as possible, so we'll stop off in Houston on our return from Italy." He gave the date and time and the hotel at which he and Kiki would stay in Houston.

"Darn!" Margaret exploded. She threw the letter and envelope at the wall. "I hate Kiki!" she said, but the hatred seemed to be mixed up with so many feelings that she was confused. She was angry at her father, but at the same time, she felt glad about him because he had given her the painting.

She crawled to pick up the letter and read again the line in which he said that he had tried to do his best. It was almost what Grandma had said about parents, that even though they made mistakes, still most of them tried to do their best.

But she didn't want to think about that now. It made her feel uncomfortable. And she didn't want to think about meeting Kiki. The thing to think about was that now the painting was hers. She looked up at the portrait of her mother and wished she could remember her—just a little. She held the letter in her lap, wondering what to do with it.

"I'll show it to Grandma," she said to the beautiful woman in the painting. Feeling comforted already, she hurried down the stairs.

Grandma was in the den, pinching dead leaves off the potted pothos ivy.

Margaret held out the letter. "Grandma, I'd like you to read this."

"Are you sure?" Grandma asked. "It's your own private letter, Margaret."

"I want you to know what Daddy wrote to me, and it's easier to have you read the letter than to tell you about it."

The telephone rang. Margaret hoped Grandma would ignore it, and she did. She took the letter and read it, keeping one arm around Margaret's shoulders. When she finished, she gave Margaret a little pat and handed the letter back to her.

"So it's all right now, Grandma," Margaret said. "The painting of my mother belongs to me."

"When you answer your father's letter—" Grandma began, but Sharon came to the doorway. "Momma, Dennis is calling from his office. His friend Jake, from Austin, is coming to Houston this weekend, and Dennis wants to invite him to dinner on Saturday."

"If he doesn't think there are enough people around here, he might like to include the A&M Marching Band, the Zookeepers' Association, and the Exxon Board of Directors," Grandma said.

"Don't you want to talk to him?"

"Not right now. Just give him the message."

"Well, okay, but he might have something else he wants to ask you."

"Then tell him to save it until he gets here this evening. I'm busy."

Sharon had taken a step toward the kitchen, but she turned back, looking puzzled. "Busy doing what? I thought you were just talking to Margaret."

"Sharon!" Grandma used a no-nonsense voice, and Sharon disappeared in a hurry.

"Your father has taken a big step toward you," Grandma said to Margaret. "Are you going to take a step toward him?"

Margaret frowned. "I don't know yet. I don't want to meet Kiki. I never want to meet Kiki! I'll answer his letter —when I think about what to write."

Grandma was quiet for a few moments. Then she said, "Thinking about what you're going to write is a good idea."

"Momma! Where are you?" This time the voice belonged to Janet.

"Here she is!" Jason yelled. He ran into the den, Debbie following so closely that she nearly tripped over him. Their words tumbled out in such a rush that Margaret couldn't understand what they were shouting about.

Janet joined them. "Quiet!" she said, and when the noise stopped as quickly as a faucet being turned off, she said, "Debbie first."

Debbie grinned. "We're going to put on a program for you in the living room, Grandma."

"Right now!" Jason said.

"I'm telling about it. My turn."

"We're going to play our recorders!" Jason yelled.

"I was supposed to say that!" Debbie swatted at her brother, who ducked behind Grandma's legs so quickly that he lost his balance. As he grabbed Grandma, she bent in two, and both of them fell backward, bouncing off the sofa and landing on the floor.

"Oh, Momma, are you all right?" Janet cried.

"Grandma, are you hurt?" Margaret shouted at the same time. Her heart was beating so fast as she bent over her grandmother that it was hard to breathe.

Grandma sat up, pushing back her hair and attempting a wobbly smile. "Don't worry. I'm fine," she said, but she rubbed her left knee. "Just give me a minute to catch my breath."

"Look what you did to Grandma!" Debbie screamed at Jason, who immediately began to wail.

Janet picked up Jason and tried to calm him. "You're not hurt, are you?" she asked.

"Grandma sat on me!" he sobbed.

Sharon, eyes wide, rushed into the room. "Is Momma all right?"

"Oh, for goodness' sake, I'm fine," Grandma said, and got to her feet. She turned to Jason. "I can't hear you play your recorder if you're going to keep crying."

He stopped and rubbed his nose. "Are you going to listen to us now?"

"Yes," she said.

"Margaret has to come, too!" Debbie insisted. She tugged at Margaret's hand.

"We'll all come," Grandma said.

"I'm trying to find the phone number for that drugstore on the corner," Sharon said. "Do you have it anywhere, Momma?"

"I'll get it for you—*after* we all hear Debbie and Jason perform," Grandma said.

She led the way to the living room. "You sit there," she said to Sharon, and pointed to one of the chairs. "Margaret and I will sit on the sofa."

As soon as they were seated, Janet began counting, "one-two—" and the children tootled carefully spaced notes that sounded vaguely like "All Around the Mulberry Bush."

Although her eyes were on Jason and Debbie, Grandma reached for Margaret's hand and held it. Her fingers were warm, but they trembled just a little. She squeezed Margaret's hand, and the trembling disappeared, but Margaret knew she hadn't imagined it.

The wrong one is going. The thought startled Margaret so much that she gave a little jump. Out of the corners of her eyes, she looked at her grandmother. There was a pleased smile on Grandma's face, the kind of smile that meant she'd rather be listening to this wobbly concert than doing anything else in the world.

But Margaret had felt her fingers tremble.

Grandma was the one who needed to get away for a while.

The thought began to take shape and grow. Margaret could stay here with this noisy houseful of people and take care of Flowerpot while Grandma went to Cancun. For a little while Grandma wouldn't have anyone she'd have to take care of, or listen to, or handle problems for.

Margaret could make it happen. She and Grandma had the same first name, so she could just cross out her own last name on all the postcards and print in Grandma's name. Then Grandma could win the contest.

Margaret was surprised that she had come up with the idea, and even more surprised that she liked it. Sometimes she had thoughts about what she ought to do, and they made her feel uncomfortable or even angry. Sometimes ideas that would pop into her head—like the idea of writing to her father—were so upsetting, she'd do her best to pop them right back out again. But this idea felt good, and Margaret found herself growing excited. For some strange reason, it was more exciting to think about Grandma winning the trip than when she had thought it would be herself.

The drawing for the trip would be Saturday. Wouldn't Grandma be surprised when she won! Surely nothing could go wrong. Not with all those postcards practically filling whatever box the disc jockey would draw from. Of course she'd win. Margaret was sure. Well—almost sure.

🌿 13 🌿

The minute the concert was over, Margaret ran upstairs.
She settled herself on the floor, Walkman earphones on.
Listening to the disc jockey's urgings to "get those cards
in the mail today!" she began the job of changing the last
name on all the postcards. She wrote until her hand ached,
but she didn't stop.

Debbie came in and flopped across the bed, watching
her write and talking to her, although Margaret couldn't
hear a word Debbie said. It didn't seem to bother Debbie.
She just kept talking.

Finally, Margaret put down her pen and rubbed her
hand. The cards were finished and ready to mail!

She pulled off the earphones. "—so when I'm in second
grade in the fall, I'm going to—" Debbie chattered on.

"Hold it," Margaret said. "Want to go for a walk with
me?"

Debbie bounced up as though she had springs in the
middle of her skinny body. "Sure! Where are we going?"

Margaret smiled. Debbie really wasn't as much of a
pest as she had thought. In a way, she kind of liked the

little girl's company—except at night when it was like sleeping with a kicking kangaroo.

"Just to the mailbox," she answered, then added, "wherever the mailbox is. I'd better find out."

"There's a mailbox down on the boulevard in the shopping center," Grandma said when Margaret asked her. "Do you know how to find the boulevard?"

Margaret nodded, but Sharon said, "I have to pick up something at the drugstore, so I'll walk with you. I really should be careful to walk every day." She studied her mother. "Momma, it wouldn't hurt you to walk every day, too. You could start with a mile and work up to four or five. Why don't you come with us?"

"Walk? I already jog," Grandma said. "Besides, there's a new yoga program on Channel 26. I've decided to try yoga. I hear it's less fattening than ice cream." She looked at her watch. "You'd better get started if Margaret wants to make the four forty-five collection. That's the last one today."

"Come on!" Margaret said. She grabbed Debbie's hand and strode out of the house. Debbie had to run to keep up with her. Sharon managed to catch up by the time they reached the corner of the block.

"What's so important?" Sharon asked. "Walking should be brisk, but you don't have to walk this fast."

"The things I'm mailing have to be postmarked before tomorrow," Margaret said. Drops of sweat tickled as they rolled down her back.

"What things?" Sharon asked.

They were just half a block away from the boulevard when Margaret saw a mail truck drive into the shopping center. She didn't answer Sharon. She just said to Debbie, "Race you to the corner!" and took off like an Olympic runner.

She was out of breath when she reached the man who was fastening the mailbags he had taken out of the boxes. "Will you take my postcards? Please?" Margaret gasped.

He held a sack open while she dumped handfuls of postcards from her handbag into it.

There! It was done! Now she'd have to make herself be patient enough to wait the four long days until the drawing without telling anyone about the surprise.

It was easier than she had thought not to tell. Grandma took all her grandchildren to the zoo on Wednesday and Hanna-Barbera Land on Thursday. Jason and Debbie kept up such a constant chatter that the only way Grandma would have been able to hear the secret would have been if Margaret had jumped up and down and shouted it at the top of her lungs.

On Friday, the disc jockey announced that they'd had an even better response than they'd hoped for. Was that because of Margaret's stack of cards? For a moment, she imagined giant trucks delivering millions of postcards from everyone in the city of Houston, but she pushed that thought away. No! Grandma was going to be the winner, and she wouldn't allow herself to think of anything else.

They spent the afternoon on a boat, touring the smelly ship channel, with Jason running from one side of the boat to the other, usually over Margaret's and Grandma's toes, while Margaret thought about the contest.

That night, as she was helping Grandma set the table and the others were watching the early television news in the den, Margaret blurted out, "We have to listen to KIFF tomorrow at noon."

She clapped a hand over her mouth as Grandma said, "What's going to be on at noon?"

"Uh, well, wait and be surprised," Margaret answered.

"You're not going to tell me?"

Margaret shook her head. She wished she hadn't told that much.

It was hard to sleep that night. She was so caught up in the excitement of the contest that she didn't even care when Debbie burrowed into her side as though she were trying to go down a rabbit hole. Margaret just tucked the blanket around them both and pictured what Grandma's face would look like when they called her name.

The bedroom was golden with sunlight when Bonnie Joy pried one of Margaret's eyes open. "It's okay. I'm still in here," Margaret mumbled.

Bonnie Joy stepped back with a satisfied smile.

"She wants you to play with her," Debbie announced from behind the smaller girl.

"I thought she'd be at the day-care center." Margaret rolled onto her back and rubbed her eyes.

"Her mother has Saturday off this week. Bonnie Joy wants to play mailman with Jason again, but I told her you mailed all your cards. She doesn't believe me."

Margaret sat up. "How do you know all this when she doesn't talk?"

Debbie shrugged. "I just know. Don't you?"

Margaret looked at her watch. She shrieked and jumped out of bed, just missing Bonnie Joy. "It's eleven o'clock!"

"Grandma said to let you sleep. You missed all the good cartoons."

Margaret grabbed the clothes that were handy, not caring that she put on a blue plaid blouse with pink striped shorts. She slapped at her hair with a brush, pulled the earphones off her Walkman, and galloped down the stairs carrying the little radio.

The kitchen was packed with people. Dennis introduced her to his friend Jake at the same time Sharon called out, "I want you to meet my husband—your uncle Andy! He missed me so much he came early this morning to surprise me!"

Gloria squeezed between them, carrying a cup of coffee to the table. Margaret shook hands with Jake and Andy, wondering if she could remember which was which, since both of them had brown hair and mustaches and wore jeans and T-shirts.

Grandma was busy putting something into a large pot, but she called out, "Margaret, what would you like for breakfast?"

"Nothing much, Grandma. Just some toast. I have to eat fast."

"Where are you going?" Janet asked.

"Can I go, too?" Debbie said.

"Find a seat. I'll make your toast."

"Here's some orange juice, Margaret. We poured a glass for Jason, but he didn't want it."

"Where are Debbie and Margaret going? I want to go."

"No one's going anywhere. You asked for an egg; now finish it."

"Margaret isn't eating an egg."

"Well, well, Margaret, and how do you like Houston?"

"Dennis, maybe we could take our coffee outside, or in the den or somewhere."

"Stop being so noisy, Jason. You're bothering Jake."

Margaret took a deep breath and shouted, "We have to listen to station KIFF at noon!"

They all stopped talking and stared at her.

"Why?" Sharon asked.

Margaret didn't answer. Finally Grandma said, "Margaret has some kind of surprise for us. We don't want to spoil it."

"A surprise! A surprise!" Jason yelled. Everyone began

talking again, and Margaret gulped down her breakfast, one eye on her watch.

Finally she said, "Grandma, could we turn on the radio now?" She put the volume on high and heard the disc jockey say, "Remember, you have only five minutes to call in to claim your prize, so listen carefully."

"What is this?" Dennis asked.

"A contest," Margaret said.

"They're stirring up the big cage, folks," the disc jockey said. "We've got lots and lots of cards, but just one big winner of that trip to Cancun!"

"Trip to Cancun?" Sharon asked.

"For Grandma," Margaret said. "She's going to win it! Shhh! Listen!"

"Ready?" the disc jockey said. "I've drawn a card. Has it got your name on it?"

🌿 14 🌿

"We have our winner—if she calls within five minutes! Mrs. A. J. Redfern on Bayou Glen Drive!"

Margaret gasped.

Except for the music that was now coming from KIFF, the kitchen was silent. "Grandma!" Margaret wailed. "I thought you'd win! Nobody could have sent in more postcards than I did!"

"Margaret, honey," Grandma said, "you entered a contest for me?"

"Yes," Margaret said. She rubbed the back of her hand across her face, splattering away the tears. "I was going to win it myself, go away to Cancun, get away from everybody, especially Daddy and Kiki, but then I saw that you needed to get away more than I did. You don't have any time for yourself. Everybody wants you to do things for them all the time, so I crossed out my last name and wrote yours in. I was so sure you'd win the trip! I'm sorry!"

For a few moments, there was silence. Then Sharon spoke up. Her voice was as gaspy as though someone had poked her in the stomach. "We don't really ask Momma to do things for us all the time, do we?"

No one answered. They looked at each other until Janet said, "Well, after all, isn't that what mothers are for? I mean, they need to feel needed, don't they?" She tried to laugh but couldn't manage it.

In the pause that followed her words, the disc jockey spoke. "Sorry, Mrs. Redfern, but your time is up. We'll have to draw another card, and maybe this time, we'll get ourselves a winner!"

Margaret gripped Grandma's arms. "Maybe now!" she said, and she was so hopeful that she held her breath.

"Ready? This next card is from Robert Pangson. Robert lives on Timbertop Lane. You've got five minutes to call in, Robert. Don't miss your glorious trip to Cancun!"

As the music started again, Dennis said, "Hey, Margaret, it's not that easy. People send in hundreds of cards. If you mail in one or two, you don't stand much chance."

"I mailed in twenty-five dollars' worth of postcards," Margaret murmured.

They all began talking at once. Finally, Grandma held up a hand. "For goodness' sake," she said, "it's really no one's business but Margaret's how many cards she entered." She put an arm around Margaret's shoulders. "You must have wanted that trip very, very much."

Margaret nodded. She opened her mouth to speak, but the disc jockey shouted, "We have a winner. Robert Pangson of Timbertop Lane. But don't go away—we've got giant, red, green, and yellow plastic kites with our KIFF logo to give away to the next ten winners. If your name is called, just be patient because you'll be getting your kite in the mail. First card—hmmm. The lady seems to have changed her name. Got married, did you, Margaret Landry?"

"Oh, no!" Margaret groaned. "Those dumb, stupid, terrible prizes! It's like being told to go fly a kite!"

It didn't help that everyone laughed.

"I'm not trying to be funny!" Margaret snapped.

"I thought it was funny," Dennis said.

Sharon reached across the table and patted Margaret's hand. "Margaret, you got that wild idea that Momma had to get away because you just don't understand what it's like to be part of a big family."

Margaret scowled at Sharon. She knew it was this kind of look that caused teachers to tell her she was being uncooperative and sullen and self-willed, but she couldn't help how she felt. "I may not understand everything about families, but I can see things," she retorted. "Grandma gets tired of all the people and the noise and all the stuff she has to do, like cooking so much and bringing people pillows and cups of tea and listening to all their problems! So she goes jogging just to get out of the house, and eats too much ice cream, and sometimes mumbles to herself!"

"Well!" Sharon said. "You're being a very rude little girl!"

"I don't want to be rude," Margaret said. "I just wanted to help— Oh, I never do anything right!" She began to cry and pushed herself away from the table. All she wanted to do was get out of this room.

But Grandma stopped her. "That was a lovely, unselfish gift that Margaret gave me, and I didn't thank her for it," she said. As she held Margaret's head against her shoulder, stroking back her hair, Grandma added, "We've all had a fine—and noisy—visit, but Margaret's right. It's time for the visit to end. Sharon will be going home with Andy after lunch."

"I will?" Sharon said. "But I thought—"

"It's time to go home," Grandma said firmly. "Janet's

going home, too. She's been missing John. So have the children."

"I want my Daddy!" Jason shouted.

"I guess I could go home now," Janet said. "If things work out."

"Things will work out," Grandma said, "if you make them work out. Dennis, it's been thoughtful of you to sleep on the floor in your sleeping bag all week, but it's bad for your back, and it's time for you to go home, too."

"I want to protect you," he protested.

"And I appreciate it," Grandma said. "And I appreciate Flowerpot, too. She's going to have a happy home with Gloria."

"With me?" Gloria shrieked. "Honest? Really?"

"Yes," Grandma said. "If Flowerpot lives with you, she'll protect you and the twos and you won't have to be afraid to stay in your own house."

"I'd sure like that," Gloria said.

Grandma looked down at Margaret. "And that leaves Margaret and me. We're going to have a lovely summer together."

"But, Momma," Sharon said, "what about that horrible man with the gun? That Bubba Gletz?"

"Don't waste time worrying about him," Grandma answered. "If he were going to come, he would have by now."

"I could stay and teach you karate," Sharon said.

"No. You've got a husband who misses you and a job to get back to," Grandma said. "And we won't need to know karate. I promise you."

"How can you promise something like that?" Janet asked.

"Because nothing is going to happen," Grandma said. "Margaret and I will be fine."

Margaret thought about Bubba Gletz, who had frightened Gloria, and she hoped Grandma was right. She didn't have time to think much about him though, because immediately Grandma began organizing people.

Margaret and Janet helped carry Gloria's things back to her house. Sharon led the twos, and Gloria—who had put Flowerpot on a leash, just in case she decided to explore the neighborhood—led the big dog over to her new home. Dennis brought up the end of the parade, staggering under a load of Flowerpot's dishes and dog food.

Next to leave was Dennis, and with him went Jake. "Are you sure—" Dennis began.

"I'm sure," Grandma said. "But you're invited to come to dinner next Saturday. I'm going to introduce Margaret to real Texas chili."

It didn't take long to pack Janet's car. Grandma put in a sack of cookies and a thermos of lemonade for the road, and Debbie and Jason had to hug everyone good-bye over and over.

Debbie tugged at Margaret's hand. "Will you come and see me, Margaret?"

"Maybe," Margaret said. "It depends on what Grandma wants to do."

"Grandma," Debbie said, "you have to bring Margaret to visit us. You have to! Margaret's my very own cousin, and I need her."

"We'll come sometime this summer," Grandma said. She put an arm around Margaret. "I need her, too."

Jason yelled good-byes out the window while Janet backed the car out of the driveway. Mrs. Fiddy, across the street, hobbled out on her porch with a broom. Before she attacked the steps, she called out, "Lots of things going on at your house, Miz Landry!"

Grandma waved and smiled and herded the others inside.

"Our turn now," Andy said. "We can be back in Austin by suppertime."

Sharon sniffled. "Momma, I hate to leave you all alone."

"I'm not alone," Grandma said. "I used to be, but now Margaret is with me."

"Oh, you know what I mean, Momma," Sharon said.

"I know it's time for you to leave, my love, if you want to get home before dark. And drive carefully."

"I'll drive," Andy said. "That's why I flew here, so I could drive instead of Sharon. You know how she always cries when she leaves, and drivers have to be able to see where they're going."

Sharon did cry. Grandma waved until they were out of sight. Then she and Margaret went inside and shut the door.

As they stood in the entry hall, Margaret said, "It's so quiet."

"Yes," Grandma agreed. "I always miss them so much when they leave, but—" She gave a long sigh, then smiled. "Tell you what—let's take a little nap, then make grilled cheese sandwiches and eat what's left of that caramel popcorn. And we'll stay up late and watch the Humphrey Bogart movie that's on television tonight."

Margaret didn't want to take a nap. She wouldn't have any trouble staying awake for a Bogart movie; so after Grandma went upstairs, Margaret decided to explore the library. She loved the slightly musty, dusty smell of the older books. She browsed among them, found one with pages that were brittle and yellowed that was all about knights of the Round Table, and took it to the kitchen. She needed an apple to go with the book. Then she'd curl up on the window seat and read.

She had just pulled an apple from the refrigerator crisper when the phone rang. Quickly, before it had even finished its first ring, she picked up the receiver. She hoped it hadn't bothered Grandma.

No one answered her "Hello," but she could hear the sound of someone breathing.

"Hello," she said again, giving whoever it was a second chance. When the caller still didn't answer, she muttered, "Creep!" and hung up. It was probably some dumb boy like that jerk she knew in fifth grade who thought it was funny to call people and not say anything.

Margaret settled into a comfortable spot on the window seat and began to munch her apple and read. She was so lost in the story of courts and knights and fair ladies in distress that the rest of the world ceased to exist. It wasn't until she dropped her apple core that she snapped out of the past. She could hear Grandma talking to someone out in the entry hall. But who? She would have heard the doorbell, wouldn't she?

Quietly, Margaret put down her book and tiptoed into the living room. A man was standing in the entry hall with his back toward her. Grandma was careful not to look in Margaret's direction as she said, "I told you, I'm the only one at home."

"Yeah," the man muttered. "Too many people here. I waited till they left. Yeah." For a few minutes, he mumbled to himself as though he'd forgotten where he was. Then suddenly, he leaned toward Grandma and said, "You're the one who called the cops on me."

Margaret was so frightened that for a moment everything got fuzzy. She steadied herself by gripping the back of a nearby chair.

Although she could only see his back, she knew he was the man who had threatened Gloria. Margaret realized that he was in no condition to be rational. Did he have a gun?

She couldn't tell. Maybe she could sneak up behind him and hit him on the head with a vase or a lamp.

But he half-turned, and she knew that wouldn't work. He might hear her and turn around before she got to him. No, there had to be a better way. Her heart pounded in her ears, making it hard to think. But one thought was clear. She had to get help.

Carefully, shakily, Margaret tiptoed back into the library and silently shut the door. Grandma, as though to cover up for any noise Margaret might make, began talking loudly to the man. Margaret tugged at the library window, opened it, and climbed out. She ran to Gloria's back door and knocked. Luckily, Gloria was in the kitchen. Margaret could see her through the window in the door. She was pouring some steaming coffee into a mug.

As soon as Gloria opened the door, hanging on to Flowerpot, Margaret told her what had happened. She used Gloria's phone to call the police.

"I've got to go back now," she said after she'd hung up.

"You can't! There's no way your grandma would want you to go back with that awful man there."

"I'm not going to leave her alone!"

"It won't help if he shoots you both. Wait for the police."

"No! While we're waiting he might shoot Grandma."

Flowerpot whimpered and wiggled, wanting to be free.

"Hey," Gloria said, "maybe we could sic Flowerpot on him."

Margaret considered the possibility for a moment, then shook her head. "Uh-uh. Flowerpot isn't exactly an attack dog."

She could smell the heavy coffee fragrance, and it gave her an idea. "Is there more coffee in that pot?"

"Sure. I always make three or four cups."

"Could I have it?"

"Why?" Gloria asked, but she gave Margaret what she wanted.

Margaret didn't waste time explaining. She ran back to the library window as fast as she could without sloshing the coffee from the pot. She put it on the window seat, then climbed back in the window. Slowly, quietly, she opened the door.

Grandma was still talking to the man. He was leaning, stoop-shouldered, against the door frame. He had turned, so Margaret could see his profile. His eyes were half-closed, and his face sagged. His mouth twisted at the corner in a kind of grimace. She guessed that he wasn't even listening to Grandma. He looked too confused. Margaret was counting on the hope that he'd be slow to react.

Margaret was shaking, but she took the coffeepot in her right hand and strode briskly through the living room. "Here's the coffee you ordered, Mr. Gletz," she said.

The man shook his head, as though trying to clear it so he could figure out what was happening. His eyes opened, and he focused them with difficulty. The gun he was holding wobbled in her direction.

Margaret didn't give him time to react. "Coffee, Mr. Gletz," she said again, and as she came close to him, she turned the pot upside down, pouring the hot coffee on the hand that held the gun and banging the pot into his arm so that the gun pointed at the floor.

With a yelp, he dropped the gun and hopped around, hugging his right hand and screeching.

Grandma grabbed the gun. "Call the police!" she said to Margaret.

"I did," Margaret told her. "I called them from Gloria's house."

The wail of sirens was unmistakable, even over the racket Bubba Gletz was making.

Grandma opened the door as one squad car pulled into the driveway and another came to a quick stop in front of the house. A television crew truck was right behind them.

"Here he is!" Grandma shouted, shoving the man through the door and holding the gun on him while the police dashed across the lawn and up the porch stairs. She handed the gun to the nearest officer, saying, "This thing may not work. It has coffee in it."

Gloria ran out of her house, yelling, "They're safe! They're safe!" Neighbors began to gather on the sidewalk. Mrs. Fiddy came out on her porch, pulling her hat down over her ears and complaining, "There's too much commotion going on over there!"

Bubba Gletz sagged between two of the policemen, and they handcuffed him, half dragging, half carrying him to the back of one of the cars. By this time, one of the men from the TV truck was filming. A woman with a microphone came up on the porch to join Grandma and Margaret and the police officers. A second television crew and some reporters appeared.

They had to go over and over the story of why the man had come back to get even, and how he'd cut a hole in the glass in the kitchen door and had come in the house that way, and what Margaret did. Finally, the police left, with one of them assuring Grandma that this time Bubba Gletz wouldn't get out on bail so easily. The TV and newspaper reporters left, too, and Mrs. Fiddy called to them, "This used to be a quiet neighborhood!"

When they were finally alone, Grandma hugged Margaret. "You were very brave, but I would never, ever have let you risk your life if I'd known what you planned to do."

"I couldn't take the chance that he'd hurt you, Grandma," Margaret said. She hugged her grandmother back, and the hug didn't feel strange. It felt right.

"You're going to have a lot of exciting things to tell your father when he's here," Grandma said.

Margaret glanced at Grandma from the corners of her eyes. "Maybe I'll write to him tonight and thank him for giving me that portrait of Mother. But I can't tell him I want to meet Kiki. I hate Kiki."

"How can you hate someone you haven't met?"

"Easy," Margaret said.

"You hate sharing your father, but that isn't Kiki's fault, is it? Be fair, Margaret. Give Kiki a chance."

"I don't want to think about Kiki," Margaret said. "It's going to be bad enough when they're here. Besides, I don't even know what to say to somebody who's getting married. 'I hope you're happy,' or 'Good luck,' or 'Have a nice time,' or what?"

"Any of the above," Grandma said. "Roger will be so glad to hear from you."

She walked with Margaret toward the kitchen, an arm around her shoulders. "I've been thinking about something," she said. "How would you like living here with me during the next school year? I don't think your father will object. I suppose you'll miss your boarding school, but I think you'll make friends easily in your Houston school."

"You don't know much about me, Grandma," Margaret said. "I don't make friends. I guess I don't really care if I have any."

"Then I think it's time you started to care," Grandma said. "I'd love to have you with me, Margaret."

Margaret thought for a moment. Then she looked into her grandmother's eyes. "Sharon was right. I don't always mean to be rude, but sometimes I am. And sometimes my teachers tell me that I'm uncooperative and I don't try to get along with people, and they're right, too. You might be awfully sorry you asked me to stay."

"Do you want to stay with me?"

"Yes," Margaret said, "I really do."

"Okay, Margaret! Then let's make a start at our new year together by grilling those cheese sandwiches and getting ready for Humphrey Bogart."

Margaret balanced the bread, the package of cheese slices, and the butter dish that Grandma rapidly handed her from the refrigerator. "But there's one change I'd like to make," she said.

Grandma immediately poked her face around the refrigerator door. "What change?" she asked.

Margaret smiled. She liked the way everything seemed happy and warm and right. "I don't feel like a Margaret any longer, Grandma. From now on, would you call me Maggie, too?"